SHADOW ON THE RANGE

Ben Foss wasn't too sure about many things, but he was certain that ghosts did not exist. So it came as quite a shock to him when he saw his old boss, Joe Kildare, late master of the Circle K and dead and buried these three months, saluting the range in bright moonlight.

Yet if the sight gave Ben a shock, it almost frightened old Joe's daughter, the new boss of the Circle K, out of her sanity. And that, Foss decided, was what somebody must have had in mind.

There were subsequent hauntings but, as the ranch foreman, Ben wasn't so much troubled by these as the skeletons that kept emerging from the Kildare family cupboard. Foss's suspicions centred on one particularly shady character from the past, and it was soon apparent that this man, too, must have an unquiet grave.

By the same author

The Brand of Destiny
Guns of the Damned
Four Graves to Tomahawk
Trail to Blood Canyon
Haven for Hellions
Killing at Black Notch
Gunned Down
Fast Guns Meet
Hazard at Thunder Range
A Bullet Sped
Gun Wolves
Sam Colt and Parson Ford
Ride for Revenge
The Gun from Prison Hill
The Stage to Friday
Gunman's Courage
The Raiders of Glory River
Terror at Black Rock
Massacre at Mission Point
The Last Town West
The Dastardly 'Rum Keg' Jones
John Scar and the Sabre
  Range
Canyon of Gold
The Haunted Prairie
Flare Up at Battle Creek
Revenge for Kid Billy
Horseman at Black Pass
West by Boot Hill
They Hanged Jake Kilraine
The Last Round-Up
Rancho Blood
Southern Blood, Northern
  Gold
Return to Spanish Hill
Blood on the Tomahawk
Cade's Gold
Guns in Quiet Valley
The Last Rebel
Gallows Bend
Dead Come Sundown
The Bloodstone Herd
Colorado Ransom

Shadow
on the Range

BILL WADE

A Black Horse Western

ROBERT HALE · LONDON

© Bill Wade 1992
First published in Great Britain 1992

ISBN 0 7090 4775 4

Robert Hale Limited
Clerkenwell House
Clerkenwell Green
London EC1R 0HT

Photoset in North Wales by
Derek Doyle & Associates, Mold, Clwyd.
Printed and bound in Great Britain by WBC Print Ltd,
and WBC Bookbinders Ltd, Bridgend, Glamorgan.

ONE

Ben Foss threw the butt of his cigarette into the fire, put his newspaper aside, and drained the last of the whisky from his glass. He yawned cavernously and, standing up from his armchair, tried to stretch the kinks out of his tall and sinewy frame. It had been a long day, and he reckoned it was nearing time to turn in. His bunk was ready, and all he need do was strip off and get into it. Yawning again, he grinned to himself, reflecting that he had never been more tired in his thirty-three years. He had figured that life ought to get a little easier for him when, two years ago, the late Joe Kildare had made him foreman of this ranch, the Circle K; but he had made a mistake there, for he did more riding in a week now than he had done in a month before and more worrying in a fortnight than he had done in a year previously. This ranch was big – so damned big! A man needed wings rather than a horse to get round it. But whoever had heard of a man with wings? Sure, he knew all about angels; but an angel he was not.

He frowned suddenly, his belly tightening. He

5

could hear feet outside his shack. Somebody was approaching fast. Then the door burst open and a woman came staggering through it. He saw that she was on the verge of collapse and, recognizing her at once as his employer, Miss Helen Kildare – dead Joe's daughter and chosen heir – Foss caught her in his arms and lowered her into the chair that he had himself just vacated, stepping back then in a rather disturbed frame of mind and momentarily at a loss for what to do next. Miss Helen did not appear hurt in any way. Indeed, everything about her appeared as neat and well cared for as usual. Yet her features were ashen, and there was a look of amazed horror in her hazel eyes.

It was obvious that she was in a state of shock, and looked in need of a pick-me-up. Upon the table beside Foss's chair stood a bottle of whisky. He reached out and picked it up, then put his free hand into a cupboard attached to the shack's end wall and took down a clean glass. Putting this and the bottle together, he poured a moderate snort of the potent spirit and then diluted it with a splash of water from a jug that was also conveniently placed. After that he put the glass to the girl's lips and urged her to drink. 'It will do you good,' he added.

Helen Kildare sipped and swallowed a couple of times, then pulled a face. 'Pah!'

'Have another swig,' Foss insisted.

She drank a little more of the whisky. 'Ugh! What filthy stuff! I'll never know how you men can drink it!'

'It's amazing what you can get to like,' Foss said ironically – 'if you try hard enough.'

'Don't you try too hard, Ben!' she warned shakily, passing a still tremulous hand across the perfect proportions of her fine-boned and classically beautiful face.

'Not I, Miss Helen,' he said reassuringly. 'A drink relaxes a guy, that's all. Helps him get a good night's sleep.' He gave her right shoulder the tiniest of playful pushes, chuckling at what he deemed to be his own silliness. 'What is the matter with you? You look as if you've just seen a ghost!'

'Ben,' she said flatly, her gaze holding his until the merriment had faded from his eyes, 'I have just seen a ghost.'

'Helen, you're never serious?'

'I am, too!' she insisted.

'But this is good old Wyoming!' he yelped. 'We don't have ghosts and things that go bump in the night!'

'Be that as it may,' Helen Kildare said obstinately, 'we do have folk who see them. And I'll thank you not to laugh at me!'

'I wouldn't do that for all the tea in China,' he assured her, coldly serious in an instant. 'You know I wouldn't.'

'I know you wouldn't.'

He guessed he'd have to humour her. 'So what did this ghost look like?'

'Dad.'

'Your father?'

'Yes.'

'Good God!' Foss exclaimed, jolted despite himself. 'He's been –'

'He's been dead and buried for nearly three months,' Helen acknowledged. 'Yet I saw him, Ben – out there – just now – riding just as he used to ride in the light of the moon.'

'Hot damn!'

'You ought not to cuss on an occasion like this.'

'Hot damn!' he repeated at a whisper. 'Helen.'

'What?'

He scratched his ear. 'I don't know quite how to put this.'

'Put it,' she ordered a trifle waspishly.

Still Foss hesitated.

'Well?'

'Aw, Brian Tuffnel, for heck's sake!' Foss blurted. 'He's such a peculiar guy in some respects. I've heard him run on some real rubbish, and your mother says he gets some strange books sent over from England. There's one about some doctor who makes a man out of bits and pieces of other men – dead ones. You haven't had your head into one of Mr Tuffnel's books, have you?'

'No, I have not!' Helen Kildare declared indignantly. 'Neither have I been alone in that gentleman's company for days. He isn't the least bit peculiar, Ben. He's just better educated than we are. You know I regard him as no more than an expensive luxury; but mother thinks I should have a confidential clerk to look after the ranch correspondence and accounts. That's why she brought him in immediately after dad's death – and I tolerate him.'

'Um,' Foss grunted.

'Shouldn't I then?' the girl inquired defensively, though a trifle aggressive with it. 'You're a bit jealous of him, Ben. He's everything you're not. Quiet, neat of person, efficient, respectful, and a tireless worker. I think he likes me too.'

'I'd advise him to go out and buy himself specs if he didn't,' Foss said bluntly. 'What is it about some fellows? Your mother spoils him stupid!'

'That's her business,' Helen announced tartly. 'Mother is family-minded, and regrets that she never had a son. You see too much and say too much.'

'Must plead guilty to the latter,' Foss said contritely. 'As for what I see, Helen, I don't go seeing –'

'Don't you dare, Ben!' she cautioned. 'Or out of that door you go!'

'Okay,' he soothed, palms raised to fend off her anger – 'okay. But there's got to be a rational explanation for all this. You know that as well as I do. No doubt you saw somebody riding out there, but –'

'I saw my father,' she cut in adamantly. 'I saw him plainly enough to be certain that it was him. I was riding towards Signal Hill. There was a path of light upon the grass. My father was riding down the middle of it towards me.'

'Glowing with cold fire?' Foss suggested. 'They always glow like that in the storybooks!'

'No, it wasn't like that at all,' the girl said shortly. 'He was just a shadow on the range. I called to him, but he didn't seem to see or hear me.

He simply kept coming. That's what made it all the more scary.'

'Did he dissolve into thin air when he got close?'

'No,' the girl admitted rather shamefacedly. 'I don't know what did happen. My horse grew balky. Then it turned round and bolted.'

'Pity you couldn't have ridden right up to that phantom,' Foss observed, 'and spat right in the varmint's eye. Sounds to me like the culprit was deliberately out to frighten you.'

'It *was* dad, Ben,' she insisted. 'I keep on telling you!'

'Helen,' Foss said, greatly daring, 'you're not having me on?'

'No, Ben, I am not.'

He stepped back a trifle, shaking his head and clucking softly to himself. 'Well,' he said after a moment or two, 'you've come to me, and it's clear you did that because you need my help. I'll saddle up and ride over to Signal Hill. Perhaps your haunter will come out and try to give me a scare. I'll warm his ghostly backside with an ounce of lead if he does.'

'You'll do no shooting, Ben!' Helen Kildare warned.

'You're the boss,' Foss acknowledged. 'But you can't kill a dead man.'

'Well, it – it could be a living one.'

'My point exactly,' Foss said. 'There are no ghosts; never were and never will be. I think you're starting to see sense.' He put the glass into her hand. 'Try to finish this. It won't hurt you, and it will buck you up.'

She placed the glass just as promptly on the table, pulling another face at it.

Shrugging, Foss walked towards the door and opened it wide, putting his head out into the night.

'Ben.'

He craned at her, legs astride the threshold.

'Is there any chance he – it might come here?'

'It was his ranch,' Foss reflected, tired of insisting on the rational and ready now to let her go on scaring herself if that was what she wanted. 'This shack, those miles of grass, the house, the cows, every dollar we spend – all was his. Why not? If my old boss is truly back, he could show up anywhere.' He switched to a more sympathetic note. 'Why don't you go back to the house and get to bed, Helen?'

'No, Ben,' she said decisively, standing up and smoothing down the front of her corduroy riding clothes. 'I want this business settled if possible. I'm coming with you. I – I shan't be frightened if you're there.'

'You really are as scared as you look,' Foss commented.

'For goodness sake!' she pleaded.

Looking to his front, Foss stepped out of the doorway. Then, moving to his left, he went to the nearby corral and, opening it, entered and caught his horse. He led the creature out to the tack rail near the bunkhouse – where he was in the habit of leaving his saddle and bridle when the weather permitted – and stood looking up at the black silhouette of the ranch house itself as he dressed

the brute. After that he swung up and nudged the
animal over to the hitching area where Helen
Kildare had clearly left her horse while she visited
him. The woman was now mounted again and
waiting for him to join her. 'Signal Hill,' she said,
trying to hide the apprehension in her voice.

Foss nodded. They spurred off, cantering
westwards and raising dull echoes that set a
nearby herd blahing restlessly. The night was
edged with silver, and the shadows of the range
ahead were thick as funeral crêpe. There was
lightning in the Medicine Bow, blue chains that
glimmered amidst summit snows, and the
distance rumbled just audibly. There were myster-
ies present, of that there could be no doubt, but
this was the earth of the earth-earthy, and Foss
still found it impossible to credit that the dead
could lie unquiet where the rich soil invited sleep.

They rode steadily for about a mile, then cut a
section of the trail to Foxpark that looped into the
Circle K's northern flank, and it was as he peered
into the townward gloom that Foss perceived
movement. Yes, there was a horseman approaching, but there was nothing weird or abnormal
about the rider's actions; and, after calling a halt
– which caused Helen Kildare to catch her breath
– he cupped a hand to his mouth and called: 'Who
goes there?'

'Brian Tuffnel!' came the response. 'Is that you,
Ben?'

'It's me,' Foss agreed, relaxing over his pommel
and letting the other man ride up.

'What's this then?' Tuffnel asked jocularly,

reining in. 'Do I rate an escort? Is that you, Helen?'

'It's I,' the girl acknowledged.

'Where have you been, Mr Tuffnel?' Foss inquired.

There was a moment of silence. Tuffnel's long head straightened on his broad shoulders, and the moon-shadowed outlines of his torso expressed a momentary offence at the nature and bluntness of the question; but he settled again as quickly as he had tightened up and said: 'Well, there is no secret about it. Helen knows where I've been. She's heard me speak of my doings on a Wednesday evening often enough.'

'He's been in town,' Helen Kildare hurried – 'playing chess with Doctor Peebles.'

'And flirting outrageously with Meg, the good doctor's beautiful daughter,' Tuffnel added cheerfully.

'Is that revelation in very good taste, Brian?' Helen wondered a little severely.

'Meg's reputation is known to be impeccable,' Tuffnel responded – 'and I was asked.'

'You've come straight from town?' Foss quizzed, in no way abashed by the confidential clerk's original hint of displeasure.

'Yes. It's only three miles from here. I have not paused once.'

'Have you seen anybody along the way, Mr Tuffnel?' Foss persisted. 'Anybody at all?'

'No.'

'Nothing strange or unusual?'

'What is this, Ben?' Tuffnel asked. 'I thought

you were the foreman on this ranch. I didn't know you had ambitions to become a policeman. I'm not used to being questioned like this. It isn't done as between gentlemen, and I'd have been somewhat shorter with you had our lady employer not been present.'

Foss knew an apology was due, but he couldn't bring himself to weaken his own position by uttering it. 'I think you've answered me,' he said.

'Am I to receive no explanation?'

'Is that necessary – as between men?'

'I spoke of gentlemen, Foss.'

'Please!' Helen Kildare temporized. 'I fear this is my fault, Brian. I was out riding earlier. I saw – somebody on the grass, and went and told Ben about it. He was perturbed; so we came back together to investigate.'

'Miss Helen probably saw a cow thief,' Foss added. 'They're always around.'

'The likely explanation,' Tuffnel conceded. 'But the Circle K covers a very large tract of country, and travellers in the night, if not apprised, can so easily trespass without meaning the slightest harm.'

'That's quite true, Brian,' the girl acknowledged. 'Ben is aware of it too. It's just that he has to do his job, and finds it hard to drop the habit of command.'

'I bow only to you and your mother, Helen,' Tuffnel said significantly.

'Yes,' the girl agreed. 'Ben has no authority over you. Please feel free to come and go as you wish in your own time.'

'I do,' Tuffnel assured her, 'and thank you for it. Is there anything else?'

'No, thank you, Brian,' Helen returned pleasantly. 'Pass on, please, and goodnight.'

'Goodnight, Helen.'

Kneeing at his horse, Tuffnel rode on past them in the direction of the ranch house.

When the man was out of earshot, Foss said: 'I upset him more than I thought.'

'He's no cowboy,' Helen reminded.

'Told me, so, didn't he?' Foss reflected. 'Do we go on, boss, or do we go back?'

'It's no good expecting you to be a gentleman, is it?' the girl said resignedly. 'We go on, of course. What's changed? We met a man returning from town, that's all.'

Foss raised his eyes to heaven, then patiently spurred onwards. He had hoped that meeting Tuffnel, after talking things out with him, would have acted as a kind of solvent and purged her mind of the peculiar obsession which had taken hold there. But, no! Helen Kildare, a realist certainly – and far from the most imaginative of women – was determined to carry this mish-mash of supernatural nonsense to its limit; and it would most likely be one a.m. at the earliest before he got to bed. It was too bad really! He could look for three or four hours sleep when he needed twice that much. Yet such was the price of his billet. The foreman could leave nothing undone; since the ultimate responsibility for everything that didn't directly concern the books seemed to devolve on him. He'd most likely have been a

happier man had he stayed a top hand, worked
his days and spent his Saturday evenings in the
saloon. But then he'd never have got this close to
Helen Kildare if he'd done that. So what the devil
was he bemoaning his lot about? He could still
afford the matchsticks to keep his eyes open,
couldn't he?

The land rolled on, filling the velvet darkness
with a pale fragrance, and presently Signal Hill
and its attendant ridges built out of the western
skyline. A perfect cone, the hill topped into
brilliant moonlight, from which the night flowed
back and down into starset. Quiet all along, Helen
Kildare, gazing upwards, was quite unnaturally
so now. Foss turned his head and eyed her
curiously. He was once more aware that, for all
his common man's tendency to doubt anything
that ran contrary to some regular part of his
experience, he could detect that something had
happened to the girl which went beyond an
immediate or easy explanation. Just as you could
tell instantly when somebody was really hurt, so
he was conscious of a disturbance deep within
Helen which had changed her, at least for now –
and perhaps forever – from the person that she
had been before. He felt that, much as he might
want to scoff at his own analysis of it, she had
encountered true evil and been subtly damaged by
it.

Before long Foss and the girl trotted their
horses into the gloom under Signal Hill. A few
clouds dimmed the moon, flying on winds not felt
at ground level, and all was a run of light and

shadow. There seemed little to see, apart from repetitions of what they had already seen time and again, and Foss, sensing anticlimax, feared that his companion might try to keep this business alive by insisting that they make the climb over the grassy benches ahead and then ride down into the outlying pastures of the Circle K. Here, as a rule, only old breeding stock was kept. It was given the chance to fatten up before being driven over to Cheyenne to ride the Union Pacific's railroad service to the Chicago slaughter-houses. To visit that herd must prove a further waste of time, but Helen insisted on nothing and sat gazing about her in a kind of daze that she punctuated now and again with a yawn.

'Yeah, same here,' Foss said wryly, ramming back a yawn of his own with his right fist. 'That ghost of yours must have signed off duty. Do I get a say?'

'Poor old man!' the girl soothed disdainfully.

'I do have to get up in the morning, Miss Kildare,' Foss responded, exaggeratedly respectful.

The girl seemed to consider a hot retort; but then she shook her head, bit her lip, and said quietly: 'Of course you do. I seem to have wasted your time, don't I? Very well. Let's turn about and go home.'

Foss was ready to do just that. The more resentful of the whole business for the girl's sudden weakness, he refused to think about any of it and prepared to concentrate on action alone. He had too much to lose – both in self-respect and

Helen's liking – to let any trace of his annoyance surface; and he had begun putting pressure on his right rein, when his horse almost exploded his careful self-discipline by tending to stand its ground. He gritted at it, pricking backwards with a skilful right heel, but the animal remained reluctant and he heard it blow softly and felt a series of uneasy puckers run through its hide. Then he glanced upwards, sensing that the creature was aware of something above and beyond him which had escaped his notice until now; for he beheld movement on Signal Hill's northern flank and abruptly perceived a rider climbing slowly in the moonbeams.

'He came out of nowhere!' Helen Kildare exclaimed tremulously. 'Don't try to tell me I'm seeing things now, Ben. Surely you can see him too?'

'I can see him,' Foss said.

'It is dad!'

The hair had risen on Foss's nape, and the breeze, a mild and virtually imperceptible presence before, blew suddenly cold on the goose bumps under his shirt. It certainly looked like Joe Kildare; the old boss had been gone just long enough for this impression of him to carry a real impact. Joe had had an erect and distinctive seat, and he had always held his reins just beneath his breastbone. The figure up there was riding thus, and the immaculate cut of his heavy jacket and high-crowned hat were sartorial characteristics which had been unmistakably Joe Kildare's.

Staying in full sight, the horseman yonder

guided his mount, with what appeared an unnatural lack of effort on a gradient so steep, up to the hilltop itself, where he turned and faced into the east – an eerie form bathed in moonlight – and, seeming totally unaware of being watched, did something which had been utterly peculiar to Rancher Kildare and seemed to identify him as the dead cattleman and no other. He lifted the hat from his head, fingers pinched into its crown, and slowly and precisely saluted the land before him, bringing the headgear down against his chest and then replacing it on his brow.

Then another run of cloud, thicker than any that had gone before, blotted out the moon and plunged the whole scene in darkness; and, when moments later the light returned, the figure had disappeared from the summit and Signal Hill was innocent of all save the shadows of the night.

TWO

Foss overslept by several minutes the next morning, and his tardiness made all the difference to his normal routine on rising. It meant that he had to do everything in a rush, and that he had neither time to shave nor get a mug of coffee into him. Others might be late at the line up – and subject to his frosty glare and sharp rebuke – but the foreman had to be there precisely on time, clear of head, exact with his words, knowing everything, and the tight-jawed figure of rule and rectitude for all to respect and fear.

Anyway, Foss was there to the minute at the line up. He had in his hands the register and orders for the day. He called the names, read out who was to go where and do what, heard the staff complaints through Arnie Hubble, his under-foreman, and righted any genuine wrongs. He finally saw everybody off for the day, ending up with the ranch yard to himself and a few decisions as to where his supervision would be needed most before sundown; but, after a while he reckoned that, as it happened today, there was little that the top hands could not see to as well as he, and

he figured that he would ride back to Signal Hill
in broad daylight and attempt to solve the riddle
of the ghost. For that, by his judgement, was by
far and away the most important question mark
in the affairs of the Circle K at this moment.
Despite what he had seen last night, he still found
it hard to believe in ghosts, and the manifest-
ation of Joe Kildare – even if real – smacked of
trouble to come. And trouble to come was the one
thing that he, as the authority figure on the Circle
K, most dreaded. He believed that, as a matter of
principle, all trouble should be stamped on early
and at source.

He had left his horse tied to the corral pole, and
was on his way to the cookhouse – to put some
grub into his belly before setting off across the
grass – when Rita Kildare, Helen's still attractive
but somewhat lined and greying mother, stepped
out of the back door of the ranch house and
accosted him. 'I want you, Ben,' she informed him
sternly.

'My time is yours, ma'am,' he answered, feeling
slightly apprehensive. 'Is something wrong?'

The woman drew him into the kitchen. Then
she shut both the back door and the one which
connected the room with the front of the house.
Nor did she ask him to sit down, but turned on
him with arms akimbo and the light of battle
barely hidden in the depths of her fading brown
eyes. 'It has come to my ears that you insulted Mr
Tuffnel last night.'

'That's absolutely untrue,' Foss replied,
honestly startled. 'Insult him I did not. Ask him a

few questions I did. There was a good reason why
I offered no explanation for doing that. Anyhow, I
figure he knew enough by the time he left us.' He
frowned. 'Did Brian Tuffnel come to you with
this?'

'No, my daughter told me about it.'

'Showing me in a bad light I fear.'

'No, she didn't,' Rita Kildare contradicted. 'She
came to my room last night – very late. I think she
recounted everything to me more or less as it had
occurred. Helen was – is a very disturbed young
woman.'

'She told you about everything she saw last
night?'

'Shouldn't she have done, Ben?' Mrs Kildare
queried. 'I am her mother. Don't take too much on
yourself – please. You are only the foreman.'

'Where Miss Helen is concerned –'

'And foremen can easily be replaced.'

'That's very true, Mrs Kildare,' Foss acknowledged. 'But your daughter is the boss. Her late
father's Will made her so.'

'It might not be wise to remind me of things like
that, Ben,' the woman said coldly. 'I was mistress
on this ranch for many years, and I still have all
the power I need.'

'I don't know what we're fighting about, ma'am.
We both have your daughter's good at heart.'

'Then don't humour her in her craziness.'

'Ah!' Foss exclaimed gently. 'So that's what you
really wanted to soften me up for. Tuffnel was just
the excuse.'

'Brian Tuffnel,' Mrs Kildare said haughtily, 'is a

gentleman and greatly your superior. You will treat him so.'

'As you wish, ma'am,' Foss returned submissively. 'But he's an employee too. Helen –'

'Miss Helen.'

'Miss Helen puts no special store on him.'

'She knows his worth.'

'Okay,' Foss said levelly. 'Mr Tuffnel's position has been made clear. So let's forget him, shall we? There's something I've got to get straight with you, Mrs Kildare. What your daughter saw last night, I saw too. I didn't believe in ghosts – and I don't believe in ghosts – but I sure as hell can't explain what I saw out there on Signal Hill. Until I can explain what I saw, I won't have my boss doubted – or treated like a silly child – by her mama.'

'Don't try me, Ben,' Rita Kildare warned. 'There's something here you'd better understand before you misjudge me and my motives entirely. For some years, as a child, Helen suffered from a nervous disorder and was often subject to delusions. She seemed to have grown out of it by the time she entered her teens, but this could herald a return of that –'

'I saw what I saw,' Foss reminded firmly.

'I think you must have been influenced by her state of mind.'

'I wasn't.'

'Well, if this goes on, Ben,' Mrs Kildare said deliberately, 'I shall feel compelled to call in Alistair Peebles. He was Helen's doctor when she was a little girl. He wanted her to go away for

treatment then, and I'm sure he'd feel the same
again today. I don't want to see my daughter
committed to a – hospital – and I'm quite sure you
don't either. That being so, Ben, you must not
humour her in her delusions. Be hard with her;
tell her that she's seeing things. We must both be
hard. Her father is lying in his coffin, down in the
family burial plot, near the stream. No power on
earth can raise the dead. Joe Kildare does not
walk by night. We must insist on that with Helen.
If she goes barking crazy, I shall have to call in
Doctor Peebles from Foxpark – and I hope you
now fully realize what that could mean.'

'Why, sure,' Foss said rather helplessly. 'I'm
clear as to what you've just explained, and I
surely sympathize with your fears, but you just go
on ignoring what I saw. I can't suddenly round on
Miss Helen. I can't tell her that my eyes deceived
me, when I've already told her that I saw what –'

'Yes, you can, Ben!' Mrs Kildare cut in, her
tones downright and overpoweringly insistent.
'We've got to help Helen whip this nonsense out of
her mind. It's for her good – and the ultimate good
of this ranch. Isn't it?'

'I – I suppose so,' Foss said, feeling his
resistance growing weaker and weaker before the
apparent strength of Rita Kildare's case. 'Frankly,
ma'am, I'm not sure yours is the best way of
tackling this trouble. But then it's equally true
that I don't know what is the best way of going
about it.' He sighed. 'Ma'am, this is –'

'A great burden that we must share,' the woman
completed for him, as he came to a halt, lost for

words. 'I'm sorry that you should have been involved. It's no part of your work to have to worry over the Kildare family affairs. But you are involved now, and will just have to follow my guidance and accept things as you find them.'

'I work for the ranch, ma'am, and, for the sake of all concerned, you won't get less from me than my best,' Foss promised. 'I'll keep away from Miss Helen, so far as my job allows, and I'll certainly avoid saying anything to hurt her state of mind even more than it's already hurt. Beyond that I guess, as those piano folk always say, I'll have to play it by ear.'

'Very well, Ben,' Mrs Kildare said. 'Just be guided by me, and I'll be satisfied.'

Foss touched his brow with his right forefinger. Then he opened the back door and re-entered the yard. Now he went across to the cookhouse and stepped inside, ordering breakfast at the hatch and seating himself at a scrub-topped table close to it. Putting his chin in his hand, he thought over what had just occurred. From the mother he could accept what had just been said, but he still had a strong feeling that the words had been spoken by one who still saw herself as the mistress of the Circle K – and that he could not accept. In his wisdom, Joe Kildare, who had indeed been a wise man, had preferred to leave the ranch to his daughter ahead of his wife. Why he had seen fit to do that, only he had known. But he had done it, and it seemed self-evident to Foss that, if deference there had to be, he must defer first to Helen Kildare and not her rather overbearing

mother. But that didn't make Mrs Kildare any the
less formidable. How was he to juggle this thing –
keep the ranch in balance, and keep his job? He
couldn't do exactly what Rita Kildare wished, and
he wasn't going to try. It would imply that he
believed Helen was not quite right in the head. So
she had been a nervy morsel as a child. Well, what
about it? Little girls were often like that. Helen
Kildare, the adult, was woman enough for him,
and right up to playing the part that her father
had so patiently trained her to play. If old Joe had
been a first class cattleman, his daughter had it in
her to be an equally good cattlewoman. And that
was in the opinion of a foreman who knew his
business, and knew that he knew it.

There was a movement at Foss's left elbow.
'Shiny' Bright, the cook, had come out of the
kitchen to serve him with ham-and-eggs and all
the rest of it – a special privilege to the
man-in-charge and, after he had grunted his
thanks to the old-timer, Foss knocked the grub
back and thirstily drank a large stone mug of
heavily sugared black coffee. He rose minutes
later, conscious of being poor company and, to
lighten the atmosphere a bit, named Bright for a
poisoner, which was a fat lie. Then, dodging the
loaf of stale bread thrown at him, he left the
cookhouse in a state of good-natured merriment;
but he sobered right down again on reaching his
horse, and he left the ranch site in a state of
gravity no less profound than the one which had
gone before.

On reaching the first of the range, he craned

over his shoulder, looking back at the rearing
shape of the stone-built ranch house, with its
patterns of ivy and wistaria and steep roof of red
tiles. His gaze fixed on the double windows behind
the balcony which served Helen Kildare's
bedroom. As he had thought might be the case,
she was there at the glass, tied into a Chinese
robe, and he saw her lift a hand to him. He waved
back, then went on at the gallop, leaving her to
guess at his mission – which he feared she might –
and prayed that she knew nothing of what had
passed between her mother and him about half an
hour ago. Anyway, in so far as he could be sure at
this distance, she looked all right this morning
and he didn't think she was likely to suffer any
form of breakdown from the shock of her
adventures last night. Yet how could you evaluate
anybody's reaction to a haunting? It was just so
far out of the normal run of experiences.

To ease his mind, Foss took in the scene as he
rode westwards. He gloried in the surrounding
mountains; they were a picture. The snowpeaks
reached back into a morning sky of the brightest
blue, while the ribbed walls of the highest ridges,
blasted with ice and white powder, appeared close
enough to reach out and touch. The effect was less
pronounced with the rocklands of the middle
slopes, and lower down the fields of scree were
still patterned with gloom, but it was possible to
see where minor slides developed and watch the
odd shower of debris vanish into the green
timbertops of the Laramie. The morning breeze
had got into the grasses of the range, whispering,

and the cows were in good voice everywhere. This
was summer, and all was clearly well with the
land. There seemed no cause for worry of any
kind, yet Foss was still burdened by his ill-defined
doubts, and his sense of oppression would not go
away. There was Brian Tuffnel too. His atmosphere kept vying for a place in all this. The man
was just a g'damned pen-pusher who'd been to
college: an upper class nobody who peddled the
illusion of superiority at tables where money was;
yet Mrs Kildare had a protective attitude towards
him that was prideful and almost loving. Why?
Foss didn't know; but perhaps she didn't either.
Women were all very well, but there was a lot to
be said for the relatively uncomplicated world of
men.

Once more Signal Hill showed ahead. By
daylight it was a somewhat insignificant bump
amidst the grandeur of the Wyoming mountains,
and it was difficult to accept the truth of that
memory which showed him the weird horseman
upon its summit and saluting the Circle K as had
been Joe Kildare's wont in the prime of his now
ended years. Had he somehow imagined it all?
Could Helen's presence have infected him with a
form of madness in that shining midnight? Now
that was a treacherous thought, and should have
been unthinkable. It just went to prove how much
he had already been influenced by Rita Kildare's
dubiously kindly tongue. For could a woman truly
love her daughter and talk as she had talked? But
a man had to believe in a situation like this. Folk
were all so different, and that was a fact.

Foss reached Signal Hill almost before he
realized it, and he found himself climbing the
bench on the immediate right of the eminence as
he decided what he was actually going to do. He
made up his mind that, as nearly as he could, he
would pass over the exact ground which the ghost
had covered to reach the hilltop. Some trace of a
shod animal's movement across grass was always
left behind when the brute was making an effort.
True, there had been an apparent lack of force
about the dark mount's climb – which had
suggested the supernatural – but, if horseshoes
had been concerned, there would surely be some
sign left, if only a broken weed, of its ascent. Once
prove that a horse of flesh and blood had carried
the dim shape of Joe Kildare last night and the
haunting was revealed as a sham, for no ghost
could ride a living horse. Either both had risen
from the vapours of hell or both still belonged to
the land of the living. No corporeal horse could
obey a spectre's touch. It simply was not in
Nature.

Dismounting at the top of the bench, Foss left
his horse standing with reins hanging loose and
walked forward in a slight, peering crouch, soon
coming to the final stage of Signal Hill itself and
starting to climb. On the incline, as upon the more
level grass below him, he found no indication of
any kind that a heavy animal had recently
trodden the area, and he finally came to the crest
of the eminence in a state of slightly daunted
frustration. Now, circling outwards from the
centre, he examined the entire summit for any

hint that a horse and rider had stood upon it
during the last nine or ten hours, but here again,
not a blade of grass had been bruised or a pebble
displaced. He could not explain it – any more than
he had been able to explain what he had seen last
night – and his underlying scorn of supernatural
forces began to shed something of the renewed
confidence in material things which daylight had
given him. Perhaps ghosts did exist after all, and
he had to do with a genuine haunting.

He gazed down the back of the hill and across
the broad plain that tilted away to the south-west.
He saw broad acres that were spotted with
drifting cows, but found no inspiration there; and
after that he let his eyes travel away to the right,
where they came to rest on banks that were steep,
rugged, and patched with berry thickets, ash, and
box elder. The highest of this land – part of the
Circle K but still an unexplored mystery to the
people of the ranch – rose into the damp haze of
the odd low-hanging cloud and formed a for-
bidding shadow which seemed to deny the
summery picture around and beyond it, and Foss
turned away from it instinctively.

But then he glanced back just as quickly, for a
blue jay, shrilling fright, went arrowing upwards
out of a clump of box elder on the middle ground of
the embankment yonder. The bird shed both
feather and leaf as it cleared the growth and went
hurtling away over the ridge, still voicing its
plaint. Alerted – but unsure – Foss studied the
point of the bird's emergence, knowing that it had
far more likely been scared by a lurking animal

presence than a human one, and he was tempted
to ignore the whole thing – as much from low
spirits and tiring interest as anything else – but
he felt compelled to justify his unapproved ride
out here in any way that he could; so he pulled
himself together and, descending to where he had
left his horse, mounted up and rode the creature
down onto the grass behind the bench, angling
right for the minute or two it took and then
putting his horse to the steep bank on which the
suspicious box elder clustered.

He climbed about a hundred and fifty feet. The
incline made progress slow, but was less against
him as he neared his goal, and he dismounted
once more beside a cluster of hickory wands and
approached the clumped box elder on foot. Letting
his right hand fall to his side, he eased his
revolver in its holster, determined to take no
chances, for brown bears were not infrequently
seen out here and an animal of the breed could
suddenly turn into a raging killer if it believed
itself hunted.

Putting out his left hand, Foss gripped a
gnarled branch and gave the elder a tentative
shake. Nothing happened, and he shook it harder,
causing the heart of the coarse growth to rattle
and rasp; then, after satisfying himself at a third
try that there was nothing to fear, he walked
round the shrubs and peered into the gap between
the greenery and the bank itself, seeing what
looked like the mouth of a cave concealed there.

Drawing and cocking his pistol now, he eased
himself past the growth and into the aperture –

his fear of that possible bear renewing itself by
the instant – but he picked up no smell of a
residential animal as he entered the earth and
soon stood erect and listening in the darkness of
the cave itself, conscious of a faint draught
indrawing upon his warm face from the back of
the place. Shutting down the hammer of his gun,
he tipped the weapon back into its holster, then
took out a match and ripped fire with his
thumbnail. He lifted the flame, and it streamed
and flickered, casting an adequate glow over walls
that had obviously been cut by human hands; and,
as he perceived particles of quartz amidst the
scars left by double-jack and spade, he realized
that he had found his way into an old mine that
probably went back into the first half of the
century.

Stepping closer to the rear wall, Foss saw the
mouth of the gallery that he had suspected from
the presence of the draught. He entered this
extension of the mine and walked slowly down it,
watching the roof and underfoot through every
yard he covered, and presently he saw something
on the floor ahead that excited him. Shaking out
the end of the match, as it burned his fingers, Foss
fired up another sulphur tip and closed in to
examine his find. Horse droppings; and as fresh as
last night. Yes, and there were too, shoe marks in
the dust. It was not too much to say that a mount
had been led through here during the dark hours.
What price haunters now? For it was a reasonable
certainty that only somebody up to no good would
have wished to use this route, and equally sure

that whoever it was had sat the only horse to be found back here last night on top of Signal Hill. After all, the disappearance of the horse and rider from the summit had required no more than that they move backwards and down from the crest while the moon was obscured. Everything became very simple when the supernatural aspects were removed, though why anybody should want to practise such an incredible deception remained as much a mystery as ever.

Lighting a third match, Foss moved on along the tunnel, glimpsing various brief side galleries and false starts en route, and he gained the feeling that, after a perhaps lucrative start, this mine had yielded little gold for the man who had put so much work into digging it. Perhaps it had become a way of life – the solace of a loner who had lost his ambition to move on – or even a hiding place from the past. Whatever the truth, Foss doubted that the unknown miner, even in his wildest flights of fancy, could have dreamed of the strange use to which his diggings would one day be put.

The matchlight revealed a corner ahead. This had been formed by the intruding granite which had clearly brought the soft rock mining to a halt. Rounding the bend – and keeping the fact of the startled bird at the forefront of his mind – Foss beheld the ring of light which marked a second exit ahead of him, and moments later he ducked cautiously out onto the slope of yellowish grass above a fairly large basin which seemed to be wholly enclosed by the surrounding high ground.

Kneeling, he passed an eye across the water
which filled the centre of the hollow, seeing a
stand of scrubby cottonwoods that grew back into
a bay of land on the further side of the pool.
Amidst the trees, and no monument to its builder,
crouched a shack of sorts which was green with
mildew and crumbling from age. At the northern
end of the shanty a black horse stood. It was
pegged into a patch of grass which it could roam
at will on a running line. The creature was
wall-eyed and of no obvious pedigree, but its
colouring made Foss ask himself whether it was
the horse; and he was rising for a slightly better
look at it, when a rifle cracked out from a spot
close to the southern end of the shack and the
bullet caused Foss's left ear to literally vibrate on
his head as it nicked away a fragment of the lobe
before flattening against the rock behind the
watcher and audibly falling dead.

Squirming back into the mouth of the tunnel
from which he had recently emerged, Foss wanted
to yell that there was no need for shooting – but he
feared the rifleman might not agree – and he drew
his Colt and looked down across the basin for his
target.

THREE

The rifle spoke a number of times in rapid succession, and Foss crouched under the whizzing lead. He heard one bullet go screaming into ricochet, and felt tiny pieces of stone cut at his face and left hand as another clipped a corner of rock on the opposite side of the opening that sheltered him. Keeping his nerve, he pinpointed the gunflashes in the shadow of the not far distant cottonwoods, spotting the rifleman crouched at the misshapen base of a woody little tree that could obviously absorb all the lead that he could throw in that direction and never know the difference; so, determined not to waste ammunition by shooting straight at it – in the hope of obtaining vital penetration – he took great care over aiming his first shot in reply, fixing his sights on the small part of a human limb that was jutting out of cover.

Foss squeezed off. He saw the sliver of thigh at which he had fired jerk back into the protection of the rifleman's tree. He knew he had missed, but reckoned it had been only just; and this seemed to be confirmed as the long gun blazed at him

angrily again, the hail of shots forcing him further
and further to the right – and enticing his enemy
just those inches out of cover that were more than
safety decreed in order to adjust his aim.

Deciding to play upon his foe's anxiety, Foss
kept on easing over to his right, content to put his
torso outside the tunnel end to achieve extra
freedom of movement and watching hawk-eyed as
the man below strained dangerously out of
protection in the search for a still clearer shot.
Holding his own fire, he let more slugs from the
other's Winchester beat around him, building up
the element of recklessness in his enemy's tactics,
and suddenly the rifleman thrust his entire right
side into view.

Now, squaring up over both knees, Foss
extended his right arm and triggered twice at the
shoulder and slice of ribs which had become a very
definite target for his revolver, and he scored at
least one hit, for the rifleman tipped over
backwards and came to rest sprawling out of
cover. The would-be killer lay still for a long
moment, then sat up sharply, his eyes glaring
hatred as he tried to get back into action from his
sitting position.

Measuring the other, Foss let fly again. This
time he scored what looked like a really telling hit,
and his enemy fell back instantly. Rising to his full
height, Foss considered the figure lying beyond
him and then began descending the slope, pretty
sure that the rifleman was either dead or mortally
wounded; but, as he neared the bottom of the
descent, he thought he detected a faint tension in

his victim's frame and this restored him to full caution. Quickly reloading a chamber or two of his gun, he circled wide to his left as he rounded the water at the middle of the hollow and thus kept his downed enemy in full view through the last of his advance.

He had cause to bless his care, for his victim abruptly stirred and jacked himself up by the left elbow, his balance no more than a great shudder as he sought to draw the revolver on his right hip. It would have been easy – from the edge of the trees and a range of only a few yards – to put a bullet in the would-be killer's heart and have done with it; but Foss suddenly realized that he didn't want that, for a man who was still alive could talk, and he certainly wanted to hear what the other might be persuaded to say; so he shot the partially drawn sixgun out of his enemy's fingers and then finished his advance on the other, stopping beside the man and looking down into the meanly graven and unshaved remains of what might once have been a pleasant face.

Sucking in his lower lip, Foss felt a spasm of disappointment. He had been hoping that his victim might turn out to be last night's 'ghost', but a man less like the late Joe Kildare would have been hard to imagine. This fellow had narrow shoulders whereas Joe had been exceptionally broad, was a mere five-feet seven to Kildare's six-two, and possessed a narrow, balding skull which lacked a single iota of the shaggy splendour of brow that had marked the dead rancher for a superior son of the human race. 'Who are you, mister?' Foss demanded, stirring the shot man with a toe. 'What's your name?'

'Go to hell!' the other whispered.

'What's the game, hey?'

'No savvy.'

'Like hell you don't!' Foss rasped. 'Where do you come from?'

'You never heard of it,' the shot man breathed, fading.

'It was you over yonder, wasn't it?'

'What about it?'

Foss glanced around him uneasily. 'It figures you're not alone, boy. Or haven't been anyway. Who's your partner? Who's playing the spook?'

'What are you talking about?'

'You know. I know damn well you do.'

The other closed his eyes and just lay there, his breathing slightly laboured.

'You need help.'

'Yeah.'

'You won't get any until you've talked.'

'Aw, push off!'

Foss clenched his teeth and scowled. He wasn't handling this well. The other was having the best of him. But how else could he go about it? In some peculiar way – that was in fact fairly obvious – the wounded man had the real force of the argument on his side. A bullet had pierced his vitals. Before long he was going to snuff it. A dying man lacked all reason to bargain. He was done with this world and its affairs. The ultimate choice was his. He could either give freely or withhold and ignore the reproaches. His was a total power. The shot man clearly intended to withhold – and to die enjoying it.

Twice Foss swung his toe. He kicked the other's weapons far back into the trees. Then he left the shot man lying and walked towards the shack which he had seen from the egress above. Reaching the structure, he opened the door and stepped inside, making a full turn at the centre of the floor. By now the tastes of damp and decay had fouled his tongue, and he spat them out, noting with a certain disgust that the shanty had been recently lived in. This was shown by the number of punctured tomato cans lying about, the ashes which filled a hole that had been dug in one of the corners, a number of discarded newspapers, and a pair of socks which had been thrown down with a needle and darning wool still in one of them. Nor was this the only evidence of habitation, for two slickers hung down the back of the door – one much larger than the other – and the reality of the bigger garment seemed to confirm the at least occasional presence of the second man about whom he had asked the dying one outside.

The sense of bafflement welled up inside Foss again, and the sheer frustration of it made the blood pound in his ears. There appeared to be a real mystery present, and he didn't seem able to make head or tail of it. Yet what was new about that? Generally, you had to take all problems a bit at a time, and he had at least proved to himself – and ought to be able to satisfy others about it too – that the supernatural had no true place in what was going on. If he could do no more than put Helen Kildare's mind at rest, it would be something. Her sanity and normal function were vital to the Circle K. Thus he had not entirely wasted his time out here at Signal Hill. He must be sensible now. Whatever the future had in store must come when it would come. Beating his brains out at this juncture would only drain him. A man must have something to go on, in order to open up an enigma, and he had nothing that he was aware of. Better forget it all for the minute – do what had to be done; move on.

He walked back outside. The black horse tearing off grass nearby raised its head and studied him. He went over to it and patted a lean flank, and the brute gave him a friendly chuck of its head and revealed itself as ordinary as he had supposed. After that he turned away from the creature and returned to where the rifleman lay. It came as no surprise when he saw that the wounded man had died in his absence, and he shut the fellow's eyes and straightened his limbs. So what was he to do? He could leave the corpse here, and perhaps no man the wiser; but the other had the right to a decent burial and to have his death recorded by the appropriate authorities, including the law itself. After all, the dead man, aside from leading a secret existence on the Circle K – which was illegal in itself – had fired on him first, and he had only killed the guy in self-defence. Yes, he would take the body into Foxpark. He should have nothing to fear from doing the right thing – while doing the wrong, whatever the reasons for it, could backfire nastily at one time or another.

Returning to the black horse, he looked around the tethering area until he found the cradle of grass amidst some outgrowing roots in which the creature's saddle and bridle had been left. There was a lariat present also and, picking this up in company with the rest of the gear, he carried all three items to the black mount, saddling it first and then slipping the bridle and bit into place. After that he freed the animal from its running line and led it across the front of the shack to where the dead man lay. Now he lifted the body across the mount's back and roped it firmly into place, talking to the animal between times, for, like all its kind, it was uneasy in the presence of death.

With the last knot tested for security, Foss stepped back and considered the enclosing walls of land, wondering if there could be an exit around that would allow him and his gruesome charge to leave here without passing through the depths of the old mine, but he reckoned that the very existence of the hiding place precluded the possibility of a simpler way in and out; so, short of trying to climb out of the basin over one of the surrounding ridges, he guessed that he would just have to ignore the unpleasantness of the inner earth and lead the black horse and its burden out through the mine.

Catching the brute at its bit, Foss set off purposefully. Leaving the cottonwoods, he rounded the southern curve of the pool and climbed the slope beyond, re-entering the mine through its rear door. Now he led on into the earth, groping as the daylight faded in his wake and, as he found himself in complete darkness again at the start of the main gallery, he struck a match and let its glow light him into the cave at the other end of the tunnel. Here he halted and, forced to go about it with considerable care – because he could see that the black mount's burden was going to get tangled up with the box elder that pressed in upon the entrance – he pushed back the growth and drew the horse out into the open air through the gap that he created between the box elder and hillside adjacent. Finally he steered the brute down the slope beyond to where his own mount was still standing much as he had left it, and then, with both animals in hand, descended the grade at a checked walk, half expecting to see cowhands in the offing, for the recent spate of firing must have echoed for miles and been audible right down to the ranch house itself, but there was nobody in sight and the silence of the area insisted that he was very much alone with the dead man.

Arriving at the bottom of the slope, Foss stepped into his saddle and then drew the burdened mount after him over the bench to the left of Signal Hill. Here he came again to the main spread of the Circle K. Riding clear of the slight barrier formed by the wall of higher range, Foss slanted north of east and rode down this course for a mile or two, cutting the Foxpark trail beneath a bank covered with greasewood and purple sage. Now he turned left, facing into the sheer majesty of the Medicine Bow and, with the mountain wind blowing cool through the golden light of the middle day, rode the pine-bordered trail into the old mining town. Once among the houses he picked up an escort of the more curious citizens, and this stayed with him up to and after he had stopped outside the law office door.

Dismounting, he saw Sheriff Amos Grant peering out of the window at him. Shaking his head, he raised his hands helplessly in answer to the other's frown. Then the lawman disappeared from the glass, and the office door opened a moment later and he stepped out through it, a lank, weather-blasted, beady-eyed man, with a slightly hooked nose and lantern-jaw. 'What've you got there?' he asked.

'A man I had to kill,' Foss answered.

'A man you had to what?'

'You heard me, Amos.'

'I hope I heard you amiss, Ben.'

'I don't think you did,' Foss said. 'The varmint shot at me a dozen times if he did once. I returned fire. Said varmint caught the worst of it.'

'I'll say he did,' the sheriff growled. 'You can't more than kill a man. Where did this happen?'

'Way back on the Circle K, Amos – in a hidden basin. I guess he'd taken up residence there, and was plainly up to no good.'

'Well, you're the Kildare foreman, my man,' Sheriff Grant acknowledged, biting off a hangnail. 'Figure him for a butcher?'

'No means of telling,' Foss replied. 'There was no sign of it around. Not that I went hunting for horns and hides – and guts. You forget things like that when you've had slugs whining around your ears.'

'Been in the odd gunfight myself,' Grant
admitted. 'Can you put a name to him?'

'Never saw him before today,' Foss answered.
'How about you, Amos?'

Grant turned up the dead man's face and had a
good look at it, spitting when he had finished.
'Nope. What you just said, Ben, goes for me too.'
Craning, the lawman cupped a hand to his mouth
and shouted: 'Hey, Dusty! Get your ass out here!'

There was no response.

'Dusty – dang your eyes!'

Now a fat-shouldered, pudding-faced man,
leaden-eyed and phlegmatic to a degree, plodded
out of the office on stumpy legs, the badge on the
front of his dirty grey shirt telling that he held the
position of a deputy sheriff. Dusty Folds was no oil
painting, and none too bright. Indeed he had
never looked the part of a lawman, but Foss had
heard it said that Folds was good at a jailor's work
and had survived in his job for a dozen years
where many a better man had not lasted as many
weeks. 'What do you want, Amos?' the deputy
asked, squinting.

'Take a look at that dead man,' the sheriff
ordered. 'I want you to tell Ben Foss and me who
he was – if you can.'

'Can't.'

'You're real helpful!' Grant snorted. 'But
knowing you I'll have to spell it out. Did you ever
see him before?'

'Yes, sir.'

'You did?'

'Told you.'

'Well, god-dammit!' The sheriff's face expressed his suffering. 'Where?'

'In the Buckwheat Saloon.'

'Tipping it down your gullet as usual, eh?'

'No harm in a man having a drink, Sheriff,' Folds said stiffly.

'What was he doing in the Buckwheat?'

'Drinking.' Folds appeared to resent being taken for a complete fool. 'Drinking and playing cards.'

'Who with?'

'That set who regular play cards in there.'

'The tinhorn – Ivan Cooper,' Foss observed. 'Piggy Clowes, Stan Forder, and Vinny Haines.'

'Bully!' the sheriff growled contemptuously. 'Well, we shall have to pass the Buckwheat on our way to the undertaker's. Ten-to-one Cooper will be playing a game of solitaire at this hour. We'll fish him out of there and let him have a look at this fellow. He may be able to tell us something.'

'That's original,' Foss remarked inconsequentially.

'You trying to incur my displeasure?' the sheriff inquired.

'I'm having a hard day,' Foss mourned, wondering what the deuce the lawman would have to say about it – if he knew all, ghosts included.

'Want me to come, Amos?' Folds asked.

'Return to your scrubbing,' Grant said dismissively.

Touching his hat to Foss, the deputy went back indoors.

'Dusty's keeping in with you, Ben,' Grant leered. 'He may need a job one of these days.'

'So may I,' Foss reflected ruefully. 'I'm right off my place of work today. I've got two lady bosses, Amos. One's not sure if she loves me and other's took the opposite way. It makes for an interesting life.'

'As well they don't know as much about you as I do, Mr Foss,' the sheriff said sourly. 'You wouldn't get by the kitchen door. Well, let's stop this nonsense. Walk that black horse on.'

Foss did as he was bidden, in fact leading a horse by either hand, and Sheriff Grant moved into the lead and stepped it out just ahead of him. They covered fifty yards or so – still shadowed by a number of onlookers – and this brought them level with the Buckwheat's swing-doors. The sheriff called a halt. Then he left Foss on the street, now standing between the horses, and shouldered through the batwings into what his companion glimpsed, over the back of his own mount, as the almost empty bar-room beyond. Grant was absent for about a minute, then reappeared with a debauched-looking man of gentlemanly dress and stance. The newcomer moved up to the corpse tied to the black horse and, kneeling slightly, looked into the dead man's face. 'Pete Boone,' he said shortly, a twist of his lips expressing distaste. 'Or that's the name he gave me. The sheriff tells me Boone tried to kill you, Foss.'

'That's the size of it, Cooper,' Foss agreed.

Ivan Cooper shrugged. 'He couldn't play poker either.'

'He'll have plenty of time to learn – and many a teacher – where he's gone,' Foss observed wryly. 'What else can you tell us about him?'

Cooper shook his head. 'He was a miserable man, and had one of the tightest mouths I've come across. I never saw him exchange two dozen words of conversation with anybody. Not that I really care for talkers at my card table.'

'Poker is a serious business,' Foss allowed. 'So there we are, Sheriff.'

'Nothing, Cooper?' Grant appealed, a little fierce of eye.

'Nothing, Sheriff,' the gambler affirmed.

'We may find something in his duds,' Grant said. 'That horse of his don't look much. Oh, come on, Ben!'

They walked on down the street for another fifty yards. This brought them to the Gothic front of Joseph Makun's funeral parlour. The fat undertaker stepped out of his establishment to meet them. He threw up his hands in despair at the sight of the dead man roped to the black horse, and murmured lamentations into his beard. Then he called for his assistants. They were two in number, coloured, and appeared from the doorway behind their master, the taller man carrying a litter. It took them a minute to free the corpse from its roping; then, putting it on the litter, they carried it indoors and out of sight, while Foss led the black horse to the hitching rail adjacent and tied it there. 'I reckon the critter will sell off for enough to defray the cost of Boone's funeral,' he commented.

'Should save the town that much,' the sheriff agreed. 'I suppose you'd like to go – being off the Circle K and all?'

'I sure would,' Foss replied.

'I'll want a statement from you some time.'

'Any time.'

'Well, I know you for a straight man,' Grant said seriously, 'and I've no doubt it happened as you told me. Some'd say I'm wrong – but sling your hook, Ben!'

'Thank you, Amos,' Foss responded; and he turned his own horse and mounted up, while the sheriff walked into the funeral parlour behind the undertaker.

Now Foss took his mount back along the street at a very slow trot. This was probably just as well, for it appeared to encourage Ivan Cooper – who was still standing outside the Buckwheat Saloon, a newly lighted stogie clamped into his jaws – to step off the sidewalk and extend a restraining hand towards the slow-moving horse. 'What is it, Cooper?' Foss asked, reining to a halt.

'Just a thought I had after you and the sheriff left me,' the gambler explained. 'I guess I didn't tell you the exact truth.'

'Exactly what about?'

'I suppose that's what made me think I'd stop you and put it right,' Cooper went on thoughtfully. 'They made a most improbable pair, cheek-by-jowl at the end of the bar. Didn't they so? Brian Tuffnel is reputed to be a Harvard honours man, and Pete Boone was about as ignorant as a fellow can get. Yet –'

'Brian Tuffnel?' Foss interrupted. 'Our Brian Tuffnel – from the Circle K?'

'Who else would I be talking about?' Cooper queried, vaguely amused. 'The name's not that common, is it? Yes, your Brian Tuffnel from the Circle K. As I said, he came into the Buckwheat a time or two and appeared to be looking for Boone. I don't suppose it means anything. Just thought I'd tell you.'

'Glad you did,' Foss said, surprised that a fastidious fellow like Tuffnel should even have lowered himself to enter a stinking den of iniquity like the Buckwheat Saloon – but nothing short of amazed that he should have sought out Pete Boone. Yet if Boone had had some connection with the 'ghost', and Tuffnel had had some connection with Boone –?

Well, a guy couldn't help wondering. Who else could Tuffnel be connected with?

FOUR

And Foss went on wondering all the way back to
the Kildare ranch. As he had remarked to himself
earlier, though nothing had as yet happened to
actually harm the Circle K, the ghostly manifest-
ation of one who had in fact appeared to be the
late rancher, Joe Kildare, must portend some kind
of trouble, and it had been disquieting in the last
degree to discover that an important employee of
the ranch had at least known a proven drygulcher
who had been hiding in a secret corner of the
spread. No matter how you viewed it, there had to
be some meaning in the relationship between
Boone and Tuffnel which Ivan Cooper had hinted
at. But what?

Again Foss cudgelled his brains until an
increase in his blood pressure set up a singing in
his ears, and he regained the ranch with the
feeling that he was unready after all to face the
Circle K's ruling personalities. The recent
development in Foxpark had added a new
dimension to both the mystery and his worries,
and to offer a simple summary of what had
occurred earlier that morning now seemed

completely inadequate. What he had so far was action without motive, and some reason for it all had to be present before serious discussion could be risked. Both Helen Kildare and her mother were demanding people, and they tended to expect too much of him.

He decided to steer clear of the ranch house for the balance of the working day. He needed the chance to rest his mind and digest the morning's new discoveries before letting his betters begin taxing him about anything that was difficult to propound. It wasn't like him to pull tricks of this nature – and he knew that he might not be allowed to get away with it – but the hours gradually wore away as he roved the Circle K's more remote work areas, showing himself to a sufficient number of cowhands for his presence on the range that afternoon to be registered as a normal fact, and nobody from the ranch house came by making a special effort to locate him; thus he reached the end of the day with his wits refreshed and feeling ready to deal with any new problems which the evening might bring.

Foss arrived back at the foreman's shack around six p.m. Dismounting, he watered his horse and then turned the brute into the crew's corral. After that he stripped to the waist and washed himself at the bunkhouse pump. Then, with his shirt on again and his hair combed, he returned to his living quarters – where he found a frowning Helen waiting for him outside the door. 'Where have you been all day?' she asked.

'Doing my job,' he answered. 'Riding the range –

making sure the work gets done. What you pay me for.'

'It's generally agreed you're a good foreman,' the girl said.

'I do my best.'

'You've been avoiding me all day.'

He didn't attempt to reply.

'You went over to Signal Hill this morning,' she accused.

He shrugged.

'Did you find anything over there?'

He nodded. 'An old mine, and a man living in a hidden place behind it. Back of the grass ridges over yonder.'

'My –?'

'No.' Foss gave his head a hard shake. 'A guy by the name of Boone, Pete Boone – as I later found out in town.'

'Town!' Helen exclaimed angrily. 'You've been to town in working hours?'

'Boone tried to kill me, but I shot straighter.'

'You killed him?' she asked sharply, paling.

"Fraid so. What's more, I found evidence there'd been another man with him. A big one.'

'My –?'

'Yes,' Foss said this time. 'Or, as I suspect, the idiot who played the ghost.'

'This is unbelievable.'

'Not quite,' Foss countered. 'The ghost was much more unbelievable.'

'But you've still no absolute proof that it doesn't exist, Ben.'

'Helen,' Foss said a little angrily, 'have you

thought this matter through. There's but one way we can finally establish that your pa is still lying where we laid him to rest. We'd have to dig him up again. Would you want that?'

'Really, Ben!' the girl announced, sounding outraged. 'You are too much!'

'Might as well be said soon as late.'

'You've been talking to my mother, haven't you?' Helen said unhappily. 'She's been telling you things about me.'

'Nothing that's made me think one jot less of you than before.'

'If she weren't my mother –'

'But she *is* your mother,' Foss said bluntly, 'and we do know that she only wants what's best for you.'

'So she tries to subvert you.'

'Hell, no!' he scoffed, fearing that he lied in some degree, if not wholly. 'She just spoke to me for a minute or two this morning. In the kitchen – and I'm the worst damned fool to be speaking of it. I'm going to end up with my eye in a sling. How can you please everybody, Helen?'

'Well, you certainly haven't pleased me, Ben.'

'I didn't suppose I had.'

'Don't you care?'

'More than a foreman should – and that's a fact. As if you didn't know it!'

'Nobody gave you permission to go to town!' Helen declared petulantly. 'That's what we got rid of your predecessor for. This ranch lies too handy for Foxpark. And you take too much on yourself, Ben.'

'Would you rather I'd left a corpse lying
around?' Foss asked quietly. 'Have you seen what
a coyote and a flock of buzzards can do to a dead
man?'

'I'm only saying you should come and report,'
the girl said dismally. 'We have the right to be
kept informed. What *is* wrong here, Ben?'

'Except that something is,' he replied judiciously, 'I'm little closer to knowing now than I was at
dawn this morning.'

'But – you *are* a little closer?' she asked
perceptively.

'Perhaps so,' he answered carefully, 'and
perhaps not. I've got to be cautious here. I must
not offend your mother. I've already put my foot in
it somewhat. I think she's set herself up to watch
over Brian Tuffnel.'

'Well, I haven't, Ben,' the girl said shortly, 'and
what I want –where the ranch is concerned – still
comes ahead of what mother wants. If you've
something to say, say it. When I think you're
overstepping the mark, I'll tell you quickly
enough.'

'I think Brian Tuffnel had some kind of
connection with Pete Boone, the man I killed,'
Foss explained. 'Ivan Cooper, that tinhorn at the
Buckwheat Saloon, told me he saw them speaking
together a time or two.'

The girl appeared thoroughly taken aback.
'Brian Tuffnel in the Buckwheat Saloon – is that
what you're saying?'

'Yes; and speaking with the guy who tried to
drygulch me.'

'That's certainly surprising.'

'And suggests much – even if it does prove nothing.'

'I see what it suggests,' Helen admitted. 'If the man you shot had something to do with the haunting, and Brian had to do with him, there could be a tie up among the three.'

'We can't ignore the possibility of it.'

'Ought I to tax him with it?'

'That's up to you, Helen,' Foss answered. 'I reckon folk are always surprising us at that. Tuffnel may have been doing no more than have a look at life's seamier side.'

'Where better to find that than at the Buckwheat?' the girl agreed dryly.

Just then an iron triangle gave out a harsh jangling nearby as a rough hand began running a tommy bar around the inside of its shape.

'Supper,' Foss observed.

'I suppose you're hungry?' Helen said.

'As ever was. Haven't eaten since breakfast.'

'Your own fault, no doubt.'

'No doubt.'

'All right, Ben,' she said, smiling. 'Is there anything else I ought to know?'

'I don't think so,' he replied. 'I can't think of anything.'

'Then go and eat,' Helen ordered. 'And don't you dare do tomorrow what you did today.'

He looked at her, dumbly asking what he had done today that so offended, but maintaining a diplomatic silence nevertheless; and the girl turned away to her left, returning to the ranch

house down the southern side of the crew's
quarters, while Foss turned away in the opposite
direction and then cornered to walk between the
corral and the bunkhouse, entering the mess hall
by its western door and lining up for chow with
the rest of the hands.

As ever, the grub was good and plentiful – ham
pie, with boiled potatoes and greens, followed by
spotted dick and custard – and the foreman ate his
fill, grinning cheerfully as he got ribbed by more or
less everybody in turn about something he'd done
wrong – which was really to say done right – and,
cigarette between his lips and coffee mug steaming
in his hand, returned finally to his shack, where he
finished his smoke, drank his coffee, and then had
half an hour with yesterday's *Laramie Post* before
closing his eyes and allowing last night's lack of
sleep to catch up with him like a knock-out punch.

He slept right across the evening and into the
early part of the night, awakening abruptly to a
shack that was full of half familiar black shapes
and bright moonlight. Yawning cavernously, he
stretched his stiff limbs; then, rising, lurched to
the door and let himself out into the night, where
he stretched again in what air was blowing and
had another yawn. Now, in an effort to clear his
head – since he still felt drunk with fatigue – he
strolled off towards the corral and, coming to its
rails, did a reverse climb up the lower ones and
seated himself on the top pole, gazing casually
towards the back of the ranch house and the
balcony in front of Helen's bedroom.

To his surprise, he saw the girl standing there.

She was peering down into the yard below her and seemed entirely unaware of his presence. Her appearance had a concentrated look, as if she were unsure about what she was seeing on the ground beneath, and he had the feeling that an incipient fear was emanating from her. Then she started back, her face momentarily plain in the moonlight as a wrenched and ashen image of horror, and a wailing cry tore itself from her lips and went twisting away into the smoky heavens about the chimney-pots. After that, she toppled against the glass doors behind her and appeared to fall in a dead faint.

Wide awake now, Foss knew instinctively what the girl had seen, and he sprang off the corral rails and ran for the ranch yard, passing through the black shadows between the buildings adjacent and emerging in the moon-washed space beyond, where, on focusing to his left, he saw a hazy male shape standing below the fallen Helen's balcony and looking upwards fixedly.

He raced for the figure, hands extended and ready to grapple, but was shocked almost to a halt as his hammering footfalls were detected and a face twisted at him which appeared unmistakably that of his old boss; indeed it was Joe Kildare's in every feature; and then the man, quick or dead, flitted away from him – as big to the inch and pound as Joe had been – and promptly vanished round the northern end of the house, seeming almost to melt at the edge of the moonrays.

But Foss wasn't particularly scared. He believed that he had heard the tread of the other's soles. Now he drove himself to the limit of his pace. A moment later he reached the angle of the dwelling behind which the big figure had disappeared. Rounding it, he thought he glimpsed a shape sliding round the front corner of the house ahead of him; but the other once again seemed to dissolve before he could be sure that he had seen anything at all, and he could only speed onwards and make the right turn for himself – feeling a real pang of shocked disappointment as he did so; for, as he gazed along the front of the dwelling, conscious that no living person could have crossed so much space in the time that he had taken to reach his present position, he saw only open garden ahead of him. The ground, full in the moon – if a little obscured here and there by shrubs and rose bushes – had no figure upon it, running or motionless.

His run, abruptly uncertain and now greatly checked, Foss moved forward into the softly glowing garden scene, trampling flowerbed and briar as he peered this way and that into every possible hiding place, but still not a trace did he detect of man or spectre; and he blundered forward and on, passing round the southern end of the house and turning down the dwelling's back into the emptiness of the ranch yard once more. He knew he ought to leave it at that – since neither ghost nor human imitation would play 'chase my tail' – but he persisted into a second circuit of the house, and again he came panting to the front of the building. This time, however, a black figure suddenly stepped into his path and a pair of strong hands caught at the breast of his shirt and stopped him in his tracks. 'What the devil are you doing out here, Foss?' an educated male voice demanded. 'This is forbidden ground to the staff! Mrs Kildare will skin you alive for the damage you've done to her garden! Don't you know better, you great oaf?'

'Great oaf yourself, Tuffnel!' Foss snarled, throwing the confidential clerk off him. 'What the blazes are you doing here?'

'I was just going to light a lamp in the library,' Tuffnel answered hotly, 'when I heard somebody with feet the size of an elephant's go trampling past the window. I promptly opened the window and stepped out into the garden through it.'

'Well, I'm going into the house through it!' Foss declared, turning towards the window mentioned and seeing that it had indeed been pushed up its sash.

'You're not!' Tuffnel warned, stepping between the foreman and the wall of the house.

Foss took a deep breath, using the whole of his will to control himself. 'Then I'll go in through the front door.'

'You're not going to do that either!' Tuffnel snapped, shoving him aside.

'That's twice you've laid hands on me,' Foss cautioned. 'Don't do it again.'

'I'll do it as often as I have to,' Tuffnel informed him. 'If you want to enter the house, go round to the back door.'

'I'm going in through the front,' Foss repeated, realizing that the confidential clerk had much the

better case in terms of the rules of the Circle K –
and that in fact he had no case at all – but he was
so worried about Helen Kildare in the first place,
and so frustrated by events in the second, that he
was almost aching to let fly at Tuffnel in the third.

'Try it,' Tuffnel rather surprisingly encouraged.

No red rag shown to a bull ever had a more
inflammatory effect. Foss stepped straight at
Tuffnel, intending to pass over the top of him, but
the confidential clerk sidled away gracefully to his
right and hit over the foreman's left shoulder,
staggering him. Hurt a little, and spitting blood
from a cut inside his mouth, Foss rounded on his
attacker at the instant of recovering his balance
and struck out with both fists, intending to end it
without more ado, but Tuffnel blocked both
punches with an expert ease and then nailed Foss
twice on the jaw.

'College boxer, eh?' Foss commented, absolutely
furious now; and this time he dared Tuffnel to do
his worst, leading with his chin, and burst
through the other's guard, burying his right fist
up to the wrist in Tuffnel's solar plexus and then
spinning him right round with a full-blooded left
hook.

The confidential clerk stood there for a moment,
knees wobbling from the force of the blows, and
Foss would have been prepared to leave it at that
had his adversary been wise enough to drop his
hands and cry enough. But, absorbing his hurts
with a visible effort, Tuffnel now danced forward,
stabbing out a straight left – perhaps as much for
effect as in the hope of doing harm – and the

punch stopped several inches short of the
foreman's nose, doubtless betraying how badly
dazed its thrower really was, and once again Foss
walked into Tuffnel, loosing two straight punches
of his own, and these banged home on the
confidential clerk's right eye and nose respec-
tively. Snuffling and partially blinded, Tuffnel
still kept his knuckles licking at the air, and the
foreman measured him briefly and then knocked
him down with a right cross, leaving him stunned
and stirring no better than sluggishly in the dug
soil of the garden.

Flapping a contemptuous hand at the felled
man, Foss resumed heading for the front door of
the house, but suddenly changed his mind and
diverted to the open window instead. In some
sense adding additional insult to injury, he threw
a leg over the sill and heaved himself into the
library beyond, crossing the room after that in a
sufficiency of moonlight and passing on into the
hall beyond. Here he expected to encounter some
kind of check to his progress from the not far
distant parlour, but none came, and he hurried to
the stairs and went up them, his hair literally
standing erect on his scalp as a terrified
screaming echoed to him from the position of
Helen Kildare's bedroom at the back of the house.

Speeding his ascent over the risers, Foss
arrived at the top of the stairs and stepped out
onto the landing beyond, diving after a few paces
more into the short corridor he knew to have the
girl's bedroom at its end. A lighted lamp hung
from the ceiling of the passage, and its beams

showed him the cream-painted woodwork and
brass doorknob ahead – giving him a clear target
for his reaching hand – and he screwed open the
door and sprang into the room beyond it, finding it
dimly illuminated by reflected moonlight and full
of black shadows.

He saw Helen Kildare at once. She was lying
near the foot of her bed, and the closed glass doors
at her back suggested that she had recovered from
her earlier upset and come in from the balcony
which overlooked the ranch yard, when some new
horrifying shock had occurred and reduced her to
unconsciousness – if nothing worse than that had
taken place.

Striking a match, Foss lighted the lamp which
stood on Helen's chest-of-drawers. Then, lifting
the lamp from its high place, he set it on the floor
beside the girl and knelt down there himself,
quickly turning her onto her back and looking up
and down the length of her white nightgowned
figure. There was no injury present that he could
discern, but Helen was ashen-cheeked and her
breathing a trifle stertorous. Raising her head, he
lightly slapped her face a number of times,
chafing her wrists and neck after that; but these
methods failed to revive her, and he realized that
he would have to use a treatment which would
give her system a more definite jolt; so he went to
the washstand, lifted the jug out of its basin, then
carried it over to the girl and set it down beside
her left ear. After that he put a hand into the jug's
cool water and splashed a cupped palmful of the
liquid into Helen's face, repeating the treatment

in a greater quantity when she didn't immediately respond, and this time she came spitting and sputtering to herself and started gazing dazedly around her, a look of sheer terror distorting her features before her eyes came finally to rest on him. 'Ben,' she said, then started to cry soundlessly.

'Lie still,' he ordered, reaching down a towel from the washstand's rail.

He gently dried her face. Then he lifted her onto the bed and settled her into the slightly crumpled place which she appeared to have occupied for a brief period at least once before that night. Now she lay with her eyes shut and her chest heaving, obviously still in a state of shock, and Foss kept shooting glances towards the door, increasingly baffled as to why Helen's mother had not come running in before now to discover what all the noise had been about, but she didn't appear and the house below remained silent.

Suddenly Helen took a long, shuddering breath, let out a groan, and revealed through her expression that she was once more her normal self. 'It was him, Ben,' she said. 'He was right here in the room with me.'

'He was what?' the startled Foss demanded. 'I know he was outside – I saw him plain – and I chased him too. But how in the name of all that's wonderful did he get up here with you? Now that is weird! I lost him down in the garden, for Pete's sake!'

'Ghosts can pass through floors and walls,' the girl reminded. 'They move about as we can't. Here one moment, there the next – just shadows.'

'Oh, don't give me that ghost stuff again!' Foss
said impatiently. 'That guy sure looks like your
pa, I grant – and I don't know how he got into your
bedroom – but I heard his feet hitting the ground
just like yours and mine when we're running
away from somebody. He's no ghost, Helen – that
I promise you! There's something well thought out
and organized going on here. It seems to me an
enemy is dead set on driving you crazy. I wonder
what for? The ranch? It can't be. There's only your
mother to inherit, and she'd surely never harm
you like that.'

'Can't you accept the simple truth, Ben?' the girl
pleaded, though her eyes held a hint of wildness.
'Dad can't rest in his grave. He must have left
something undone in this life. We've got to find
out what it is, and do it for him. He'll never lie
quiet otherwise.'

'Rubbish!' Foss assured her as kindly as he
could, gazing around the bedroom for a possible
way in other than the normal entrance and the
balcony, and he saw a closet in the wall on the left
of the bed. 'I'm going to have a look in there,
Helen.'

'There's no need,' she said. 'It's empty.'

Ignoring her words, he walked round to the
closet and opened its door. He saw at once that it
was indeed empty, though there were lines of pegs
for clothing across its back and along its sides.
The walls appeared pretty solid, and the faint
smell of dust which issued from the interior
suggested that it had not been opened in some
considerable time. No, how the haunter had got in

remained a mystery. But then Helen might not have seen the phantom up here at all. God alone knew what state her mind was in. She might have imagined everything she had told him!

Shrugging, he pushed the door shut and turned away from the closet. Then, as he heard rapid footfalls approaching the bedroom from the landing, he looked towards the door and felt a spasm of apprehension as Helen's mother entered. Rita Kildare's eyes were blazing, and fury was shaking her from head to toe. Indeed, so enraged was she that she could not speak for a few moments, but stood there hooking her thumb at the door and mouthing words that would not come. But finally she managed to splutter out: 'You're fired, Ben Foss! Get out of here! Get off this ranch! Go!'

This was one of those occasions when asking for reasons was bound to prove a waste of time. Anyway, Foss was tolerably sure that he could supply his own answers; and he prepared to leave the room.

FIVE

Foss had taken only two steps towards the door, when Helen Kildare sat up sharply on her bed and called: 'You stay exactly where you are, Ben!'

'Just get out of here, damn you!' the girl's mother raved.

Halting, Foss shared a frown between the pair of them and said: 'I'm not an old slipper you ladies can rip in two. What's it to be?'

'Mother,' the girl snapped, 'I reserve the right to hire and fire on the Circle K. If Ben deserves to be discharged, I'll discharge him. But first I want to hear what this is all about.'

'You should see what that wicked man has done to Brian!' Mrs Kildare choked out. 'He's split the poor boy's right eye and, I think, broken his nose! Brian is an ugly mess! His good looks are ruined! He'll never be the same again!'

'Ben?' Helen asked.

'There was a bit of a fight out front,' Foss admitted. 'Tuffnel fancies himself as a boxer. I learned to fight a different way. Tonight mine was the winning way. Tuffnel asked for it.'

'What was the fight about?' Helen demanded.

'I was at the front of the house,' Foss explained, 'trying to get in to reach you – because I knew you were in need of help. Tuffnel got between me and the door. I asked him to get out of the way, and he wouldn't.'

'Who struck the first blow, Ben?'

'He did,' Foss answered bluntly. 'But I was glad of the chance to answer it. I'll share the blame with that stuffed-shirt, Helen, but I won't take it all.'

'I don't know, Ben,' Helen said unhappily – 'I really don't know. When the foreman starts setting about people, it does begin to look like time for –'

'How if it had been some disagreeable cowboy?' Foss inquired angrily. 'That'd have been all right, I suppose. No harm in giving a no-account boy who knows little better a hiding, but the same thing's a horse of a different colour when it's a college boy overstepping the mark. I know he belongs to the house, but he's also ranch staff, and he started it. I was thinking of you – and only you! – at rock-bottom. If I was wrong in that, then fire me. Because frankly, ladies, I've got troubles enough and don't want to work for such a crazy, mixed up organization. There, I've said it; and I mean it.'

'I confess, Ben,' Helen said reluctantly, giving her mother a rather accusing glance, 'I was mighty glad to see you. I had cried out loud enough, and I was starting to wonder whether anybody cared.'

'I don't know what's up with you, Helen,' Rita

Kildare responded waspishly. 'You're beginning to behave again just as you did when you were a little girl. I have to warn you, daughter – and I've already spoken to Ben Foss about this – that if this goes on, I shall have to call in Doctor Alistair Peebles from Foxpark. He was your doctor in the old days and understands your trouble. Honey, it could result in your having to go into a sanatorium.'

'Is it possible,' Helen asked, sounding very hurt, 'that you want to see me driven mad and certified insane?'

'Don't be ridiculous, Helen!' Rita Kildare exploded. 'It seems some strange mania has got hold of you. I want to see you cured, that's all. If the strain of running this ranch is your trouble, my love, take a long holiday – go anywhere you like. I'll look after things while you're gone. There's no reason why you should ever work again if you don't want to. God knows! We have money enough in store for you to live like a lady for the rest of your days – living anywhere you please and just visiting us when you've the mind to. What do you say?'

'Don't be ridiculous!' Helen answered, throwing the words her mother had recently used back into her teeth. 'Dad left me the task of running this ranch, and I'm going to do it right through to the end.'

'Which could be a mighty unfortunate one for you, my girl,' Rita Kildare declared, 'if you go on as you have been going! Why, Helen, you're already seeing things! Well, aren't you?'

'I have to tell you again,' Foss protested – 'that one won't do! What your daughter's seen, Mrs Kildare, I've seen too. And not so long ago at that. I saw a guy who looked almighty like the old boss standing under Helen's balcony and pretending to be a ghost. G'dammit! If I ever get a hand into that old sidewinder's collar, I'll put my boot against his backside so's he'll remember! It sure is a good act he puts on, but it is an act – and there's some dark wickedness behind it, I'll swear! If Brian Tuffnel's a genuine friend of this ranch, I'd like to have him prove it. He's been seen keeping some mighty low company for the fine gentleman he pretends to be!'

'You continually go too far!' Mrs Kildare snapped. 'You're jealous of your betters, Ben Foss – and that's enough!'

'There's some excuse for how Ben feels, mother,' Helen explained. 'A man tried to kill him today. That man had been seen in town – in the Buckwheat Saloon – speaking with Brian Tuffnel.'

'Birds of a feather, ma'am,' Foss reminded.

'Lies!' Mrs Kildare stormed. 'I don't believe a word of it! Brian would never demean himself by visiting a cesspool like the Buckwheat!'

'Ivan Cooper, the gambler at that saloon, will tell you different,' Foss assured her. 'But right now it still proves nothing. I suggest – if you want my help – we start trying to prove something. If you ask me, everything points to somebody trying to change the rule on this ranch, and I don't believe there's a great deal more to it than that. An unknown person – who has to be close to you,

Helen – wants you out. Anywhere. Into a lunatic
asylum or some fancy hotel on the other side of the
Atlantic Ocean. Makes no never mind. If I've read
it aright, you're in the way of power and ambition.
It figures somebody doesn't like the arrangement
Joe Kildare left behind him.'

'Is it possible that you're accusing me of something untoward, Ben Foss?' Mrs Kildare asked
narrowly.

'I haven't mentioned your name,' Foss retorted.

'If the cap fits –?'

'Your words again, ma'am.'

'Stop being silly, mother!' Helen ordered. 'What
other ideas have you got, Ben?'

'It goes without saying that it's somebody who
looks like your late father who's playing the ghost,'
Foss said. 'I've been told Joe Kildare was the last
male of his line. Is that true or false?'

'You know it's true,' Helen said. 'Dad never made
any secret of it.'

'You are sure about it?'

'Of course she's sure!' Rita Kildare scoffed.
'Ghosts, for goodness sake! What a silly pair you
are!'

Foss ignored the older woman. 'If a blood
relation can't be involved, then it's either got to be
an actor at work or somebody of similar build who
probably knew Joe Kildare well.'

'It strikes no chord,' Helen said.

'We're not exactly at the forefront of modern life
here,' Foss observed. 'During the time that I knew
him, your father didn't travel far or have much of a
social life. How often would you say he got

photographed?'

'Privately?'

'For preference. Since it could indicate a friend.'

'Never. He regarded photographs as a vanity.'

'Publicly? For a newspaper, say?'

'Not in years, Ben,' Helen responded. 'Why do you ask such a question?'

'Well, anybody who puts on a disguise, in the circumstances I'm thinking about,' Foss explained, 'has to have a model to work from. If not the man himself, some form of likeness. A photograph must suit best.'

'Joe might have been photographed anywhere and at any time,' Mrs Kildare said, the note of mockery still in her voice. 'You remind me of a child making up a game. All this is so vague and improbable.'

'I don't see that,' Foss said. 'Though I must admit it doesn't help a lot if no memories are stirred. I have to do the best I can – kick around whatever's there. It's all improbable, ma'am – implausible, and hell, downright unbelievable; but maybe that's its very strength. You can't go running to the law with a haunting. Chances are, the sheriff will warm your seat with a load of buckshot. But if you don't see, you don't, and that's that.'

'What else, Ben?' Helen asked.

He thought hard, but nothing obviously relevant came to mind, and he finally shook his head. 'I'm sure you'll do your own thinking before you go to sleep. Perhaps you'll come up with something helpful when you wake.'

'It's a mystery we've got to solve for ourselves,' Helen agreed. 'What you just said is true. We can't go running to the law with something like this.'

'Not as it stands,' Foss acknowledged. 'But isn't there still a matter that you ladies have to settle between you? Do I still work for the Circle K or have I been fired?'

'Of course you still work for me,' Helen said firmly. 'Mother?'

'All right, my dear,' Rita Kildare capitulated. 'You do have the right to hire and fire. But if I had my way, Ben Foss would be off this ranch first thing tomorrow morning and no reprieve. What he did to Brian is unforgivable!'

'Oh, what's so unusual about two men punching each other?' Helen inquired. 'Men have been fighting on this ranch ever since I can remember. It will do Brian Tuffnel no harm at all to have discovered that there is somebody on the Circle K who puts my welfare ahead of everything else.'

'Okay,' Foss said, 'let's leave it at that. I bid you goodnight, ladies.' He walked out of the bedroom and into the short passage beyond. Here he was immediately struck by an afterthought and halted again. Then, leaning backwards, he thrust his head into the girl's bedroom again and added: 'Helen, I'd sleep with a gun for company. That big forty-five of your dad's should do a treat. I suspect it would blow a master hole through that ghost of ours.'

Neither Helen nor her mother made an answer, and Foss resumed his departure. He crossed the landing and descended the stairs; then, re-entering the library, stepped out through the window that was still open there and came to a stop in the moonlight. Once more he gazed around the faintly gleaming garden, again asking himself how the figure that he had chased could possibly have vanished during the few moments that it had been out of his sight while he had traversed the northern end of the house and then reappeared in Helen's bedroom so soon afterwards. That one had still got him beaten, and his scalp crept a little when he thought about it. He remained convinced that there was a logical explanation for all that had happened, but he wished he could settle on what it was.

Now he walked back round the northern wall of the dwelling, heading for the foreman's shack and promising himself as he went that he would return to the front garden at sunup and make a thorough examination of the ground there. He was already certain that he would find something to dissipate his doubts – for there was a faint stirring in his memory that he could not enhance just now – but all that was for when he had rested and the daylight had returned.

Regaining his shack, he undressed and went straight to his bunk, expecting to drop off at once – regardless of the earlier sleep that he had taken in his chair – but he found himself still uneasy about Helen Kildare, for, though his recent actions had been so sure, there was no guarantee that the haunter would not visit her again. He reckoned that she would be all right if she took his advice and kept a pistol handy. But he feared her mother might not allow that. Anyway, he couldn't protect Helen every moment of the time and she would have to look for strength inside herself. She had never lacked nerve in the past, and always risen to the test. She was a big person – as her father had judged her to be – and growing. If only he could fully trust that mother of hers; but he couldn't. Instinctively, he felt there to be a flaw in the mother/daughter relationship, and the feeling grew stronger by the minute. Rita Kildare could not be entirely innocent of what was going on; she was too close to it all – her influence permeated everything; and Foss's subconscious shied from the shadow of her guilt.

Presently he slept, but it was a sleep full of confused dreams, and he awoke with a knotted stomach and a light sweat upon his brow. Once more he rose thick-headed and full of yawns, but a thorough sluicing under the pump fully awakened him to the memory of what he had last planned the night before; and he had just begun walking back to the front garden again, when the sound of a hard-ridden horse coming in from the west checked him near the corral and caused him to crane sharply.

He saw a plump man on a big red horse moving towards him, and was instantly apprehensive, since he didn't normally see this particular man and his beast for weeks on end – only, indeed, such times as he drove the waggon carrying supplies out to the line shack which the rider occupied on the western border of the Circle K. There had to be something seriously wrong out yonder, for Walt Leonard would never dream of galloping the eight miles back to the ranch house in normal circumstances. Aside from his responsibilities on the line – and he was conscientious enough – Walt had a soft pelt and hated the damage done him by fast movement for any longish period in the saddle. Doubtless, judging from the lathered state of his horse, he had all but skinned his rear by now and was suffering a private torment that was better not thought about. 'Whoa up, Walt!' Foss shouted cheerily, intent on keeping it as light as he could. 'You and that sauce-splashed cayuse will never make it through the day!'

Walt Leonard reined back hard. His horse anchored up on all four, the shoes sliding close together, and the brute came skating to a halt only yards short of the foreman. Leonard swung his right leg up and over, then dropped whole-footed to the ground. Wincing, he lumbered towards Foss, wheezing even worse than his overtaxed mount. 'Ben!'

'Yes?'

'Glad I found you so quick. We got trouble, boy!'

'Guessed it.'

'Rustlers!'

'That's a rare one.'

'Hit at moonset, the cheeky varmints!' Leonard explained. 'Right close to the shack. I actually heard 'em on the rob – and went for them with my gun – but they were several, and I remembered your rule about first staying alive and getting the word home. So I stayed alive, and here I am, telling you.'

'I see – and hear you,' Foss acknowledged. 'What did they get, Walt?'

'How can I answer that for sure?' Leonard asked aggrievedly. 'It's dark when the moon goes down. I turned a dozen steers back across our line yesterday evening, and I figure that bunch of thieves snapped 'em up at Bill Sherman's price.'

'You're sure those steers were ours?'

'I know our brand when I see it!' the plump cowboy snorted, pink cheeks turning a darker shade of red. 'If you think I'm blind or daft, what'd you put me out there for?'

'Simmer down, Walt,' Foss advised. 'If you weren't up to a line job, you wouldn't be there. I have to ask. It's easy to make mistakes over brands at the end of the day. We don't want any hollering matches with our neighbours. Jock Farnes and Trig Muldoon have got mouths enough on them, and little ranchers love it when they can seem to prove that big ones are thieves. But if you're sure, you're sure.'

'I'm sure,' Walt Leonard said confidently. 'What are you going to do about it, Ben?'

'Get the critters back, of course,' Foss responded. 'Catch yourself another horse from among the spare mounts in the small corral. Your fellow will never keep up when we gallop back west.'

'Okay.'

'I'm going to dig some boys out of the bunkhouse,' Foss said. 'Be with you again shortly.'

'Bring the guys who can shoot straightest!' Leonard called.

Foss nodded, but more to himself than the

pink-cheeked cowboy. As a rule, threatened by men in pursuit, rustlers broke up and ran for it; but just once in a while a desperate band would decide to fight for their stolen beef and open fire. When that happened, members of the chase could get hurt, and it was a great help to have men among the pursuers who could promptly return the shots and give better than they received. He would certainly take the Circle K's best guns with him – and hope eventually to pack a couple of dead cow thieves into Foxpark. Nothing deterred would-be rustlers like a corpse or two on display in the undertaker's window. It gave a man to think. First the haunting – and now this. It never rained but it poured!

The foreman put his head into the bunkhouse. He saw the drowsy hands, newly washed and dressed, sitting around on their beds and having a scratch while they waited for the breakfast call. Foss summoned a dozen of the crew to him, then quickly told the men what they were needed for. Glad of the excitement in prospect, the cowboys selected tumbled out of their quarters, and Foss walked after them, checking his revolver as he went.

It took only a short while to saddle up and, as it appeared unnecessary to provision the group – since the rustlers could hardly have driven their stolen cattle that far afield as yet – Foss was able both to prepare his own horse and shout for Arnie Hubble, the under-foreman, to carry word of what he was undertaking to the ranch house. Then, not twenty minutes from the moment that Walt

Leonard had arrived at the buildings, Foss gave the order to move out.

Now it was all ride. The horsemen streamed westwards, noisy with resolve. Seeing so many figures around him, Foss wondered whether he had overstaffed his pursuit – which could mean that he was robbing the ranch of men needed for more ordinary jobs – but he had always believed that it was better to be sure than sorry. If it should come to a shooting match, he ought to have enough men with him to surround the enemy. With that done, there could be no escapers and the fight that much sooner finished.

The range stretched westwards. As ever, it was a place of flying light and racing shadows. Black birds swept down country with the horses, calling. It was not yet the time of morning dews, and yesterday's heat rose from the trampled grass and formed a sweaty, humid vapour that clung. Keeping his eyes to the fore, Foss surged into the lead – shouting for Walt Leonard to ride with him – and now he seldom looked to either hand.

Before long Signal Hill and its supporting ridges loomed ahead. The horsemen surged over the barrier and streamed down the other side, entering the last pastures of the Kildare spread. They passed through the slow drift of the market herd on the ample graze, and soon brought Walt Leonard's line shack in sight. The mounts were sweating now and slowing also, but that did not matter much, for the party was nearing the point where the real pursuit would begin and slower progress become inevitable.

Pushing on beyond the line shack, the party entered the less verdant areas where the Circle K ended. At this stage, on the foreman's word, Walt Leonard began to bawl general directions and point a chubby finger when necessary. But the tracks left by the rustlers were fairly obvious hereabouts and it was easy to follow their sign for the next mile or two. After that, however, the trace got lost amidst outcrops of rock and it was needful to rein down to a walk and call on a man named Bart Swayzee, the best tracker present, to find it again and indicate the way forward. In this fashion the pursuit – which met with a number of similar checks – was constantly renewed.

Ahead the horizon heaved darkly against the duck-egg blue of the sky. Grassy hollows, naked ridges, and stands of pine trees went to meet it. Water pooled in places, ripples blowing across its shining surfaces, and wings of aspens took their streaming yellow presence into the corners of the scene. Foss sensed the increasing wildness of the land, and was beginning to fear that this business was going to take longer than he had bargained for, when a cluster of steers became visible at the base of a large but shallow depression ahead of them and Walt Leonard uttered the foreman's own immediate thought as he yelled: 'Them's our critters, boys!'

'Aw, them thieves have already give up and gone!' another man observed disgustedly. 'Ain't it always the doggone same? And me with this rope knotted and ready!'

'Use it to do your job, Perkins!' advised the

foreman, gazing around him, both high and low, for he couldn't believe in the simple analysis which had just been uttered and was filled with an uneasiness that quivered in his hands and disturbed the rhythm of his heart. It was all too pat; rustlers didn't quit that obligingly. True, they could have had somebody watching their backtrails for any sign that they might soon be overtaken, but Foss got the impression from the cattle below – which were settled and grazing placidly enough – that they had been abandoned here some time ago by men who had left them for a deliberate purpose.

The horsemen closed on the animals, and Foss was the first among them. Circle K brands were evident on every haunch. Walt Leonard had indeed made no mistake about that. Grinning mechanically, Foss swung down, for there was an old red bull present that he had known for years and found to be of a most friendly disposition. 'Hi, mister!' he greeted, walking up to the brute's head and giving it a pat on the neck. 'Long time no see, eh? Going to tell me all about it?'

A shot cracked out. The bullet shattered the tip of the bull's left horn which was covering Foss's breastbone, and the lead was sufficiently diverted to rip through the slack of the foreman's shirt, just missing the flesh of his left side before emerging above his hip.

In the same split instant he realized that the stolen beeves had been no more than a cunning lure. This attempted bushwhacking had been the reason for it all. And it made him wonder what might be happening back at the ranch.

SIX

Foss lifted his eyes. Blue smoke pinpointed the spot from which the shot had come. It was near the top of the depression's western wall and behind a pile of rocks. Now he saw movement up there. A man sprang to his feet, rifle at the port, and started running towards the lip of the hollow above him. Jerking his revolver, Foss triggered three rapid shots after the fleeing man, but failed to score a hit – as did those of his companions who also opened fire – and the rifleman passed over the rim of the low and out of sight among the trees and boulder-heaps that covered much of the land beyond. 'We going to chase him, Ben?' Walt Leonard demanded excitedly.

Foss gave his head a decisive shake. 'No.'

'Why the hell not?'

'Because I say so, pal,' Foss responded, grinning to take the sting out of his words, since he perceived that Leonard's concern was all for him. 'We've got our beeves back. That's what matters to us. I'm not sending guys into a situation where the advantage must lie with a hunted sharp-shooter. Damned if I'm about to buy a new black suit for the funeral of any galoot here. That would be sheer waste!' He rubbed at the tip of his nose, then patted the no more than slightly startled red bull's neck again. 'All right, boys. Two of you had better hang back and help Walt Leonard drive these steers back onto Kildare grass. The rest of you can follow me back to the ranch. It wouldn't surprise me if our cook has hanged himself by now over our spoiled breakfast. It'll get eaten all the same. I know you guys were all born with cast-iron guts. Come on!'

Remounting, Foss turned his horse about and then led out of the hollow, travelling just to the left of the climbing sun. Holding to a steady canter, he led the slightly reduced ranch party back onto the Circle K, and they persisted in their ride thereafter until they regained the main corral. Here they dismounted and tied their horses to the rails. Then the cowboys headed for the mess hall and their delayed meal, while Foss walked on into the ranch yard and approached the back of the house. With each step he took, he anticipated an eruption from the dwelling that would fulfil the fear of disaster which had bothered him since he had been fired on; but nothing of the kind happened, and his knock on the back door brought Mrs Kildare to it within moments. The smell of baking was in her garments, and a small amount of flour fell from her hands as she dusted them off. 'Well?' she asked.

'Hubble told you about the rustled cows?'

'Yes. Did you recover them?'

'We did, ma'am,' Foss answered respectfully. 'They should be back on the Circle K by now.'

'And the rustlers?'

'They high-tailed — before we could catch up with them,' Foss explained, eyeing the woman narrowly for any hint that she had been directly implicated in the attempt to draw him far afield and murder him, but no suggestion of guilt appeared in her face and he saw no reason to go into the matter of the bushwhacker.

'You didn't have them pursued?'

'No, ma'am. Too risky. Besides, live cowhands do more work than dead ones.'

'Very sensible,' Rita Kildare acknowledged curtly. 'I'll speak to the sheriff about this incident when I'm next in town.'

'Just as you wish, ma'am,' Foss assured her. 'Is Helen all right this morning?'

'Of course she's all right,' the woman responded sharply. 'Why shouldn't she be all right? I told you that we mustn't give in to those silly notions that she sometimes has. She's up in her room, going through her accounts. Let her play boss while mother does the baking, eh?'

'As best suits,' Foss agreed pleasantly.

'You had better go and get your breakfast, Ben.'

He nodded, and Mrs Kildare shut the door. Turning on the step, he looked towards the crew's quarters, but then recalled his plan of last night to examine the front garden by daylight and faced north. Striding off, he rounded the end of the house and soon came to the dwelling's eastern prospect.

Foss began his inspection immediately. Going
at it both openly and systematically, he kept his
eyes low and walked slowly back and forth over
the dug ground, still far from sure of what he
sought but knowing that there was something
present which was all-important to exposing the
haunting as a sham. Abruptly sensing a presence
at a nearby window, he used the corner of his
right eye to glimpse Brian Tuffnel's lopsided face
behind the glass. He had no power to stop the
other from watching him, and simply ignored the
man. Disturbed by Tuffnel's stare nevertheless,
Foss concentrated even harder than before, and it
was about then that the thought which had
refused to come through during the night
manifested as a memory of an object seen years
ago and dismissed as a fairly normal presence of
no consequence.

He went at once to the ground along the base of
the house adjacent; and here, hidden by the
overhanging branches of two lilac trees, came
upon a wooden door which had sunk with the
years until it lay an inch or so beneath the level of
the surrounding earth. What he beheld was
undoubtedly the way into a root cellar. Hunkering
over the sunken woodwork, he took in the full
details of its deterioration; then, far more
importantly, the evidence that it had been opened
recently more than once; for the baked soil which
had lately filled its setting now lay about it in
broken strips of what looked like a black crust. He
could also make out scratches which were bright
and new in the rustiness of three big hinges that

had been long at the mercy of the weather and not received the benefit of oil or cleaning in a decade, while the final proof of recent disturbance lay in the torn up and flattened weeds to the left of the covered opening, which showed where the door had been thrown back and come to rest on the ground, pressing down all the growth that had got in its way.

Rising a little, but still bent at the knees, Foss thrust his fingers under the bottom of the door and put out a good deal of his strength – far more than was required as it happened; for the woodwork was not unduly heavy, neither locked nor bolted, and turned cleanly on its hinges, rising to fall back on the oblong of crushed weeds and such that it had flattened before. For the rest, a black hole – with steps descending into it – now yawned before him, and an odour of crumbling brickwork and damp soil rose to fill his nostrils.

Moving cautiously – and still ignoring the face at the nearby window – Foss now walked down the steps into the cellar, the daylight shrinking about him as he descended and the earthy darkness closing out every detail of the underground chamber that he had entered as his soles found bottom. Rummaging in a trouser-pocket, he located and took out a match, firing the sulphur with a flick of his thumbnail, and flame blossomed, its light revealing the rotten shelves around the dust-caked walls, a ceiling where cobwebs festooned, and a second flight of steps over to the right that rose to a door which obviously connected the cellar with the house

above. Walking now to this second stairway, Foss
held his match to the risers, seeing big footmarks
in the dust upon them. He then noted that,
intermingling with this first set of tracks, was a
slightly smaller one, each smudging the other by
turns and providing a perfect picture of shared
movement up and down. For two men had clearly
used these steps a number of times recently, and
Foss had no doubt that they had been the ghost
and the ghost's assistant; since it was now plain to
him that the weird individual whom he had
chased in the night had been able to disappear so
quickly from the garden thanks to the helper who
had been standing guard over the exterior entrance
to the root cellar – from which last night's
haunting had almost certainly originated – and
been ready to close up behind him the instant that
they were both safely back into their hiding place
under the foundations of the ranch house.

So, though the identity of the ghost still
remained a mystery, Foss was near enough
certain that the helper had been Brian Tuffnel.
Small wonder that the confidential clerk had later
emerged from the library window to intercept him.
The fellow had simply put himself in place to
confuse and divert in case luck or inspiration
should have taken the seeker at once to the root
cellar which the ghost – who would by then have
climbed into the upper house to haunt Helen's
bedroom – had undoubtedly planned to use as his
hiding place once again after completing his
terrifying mission upstairs. Further proof of how
close his enemies must have felt that he, Foss,

had come to upsetting their plans entirely had to be seen in the bushwhacking attempt which must have been arranged at the night's end – though whether by Tuffnel or the ghost himself was as yet, of course, impossible to say.

Wondering what precisely was situated above the inner flight of steps, Foss struck a second match and began climbing it, and he had just reached the small landing in front of the door at its top, when an object came sailing in through the garden entrance to the cellar and thudded to rest on the floor below, hissing and spitting in an obnoxious manner and giving off sparks that stank of nitrates.

Dynamite! Of all things! Somebody – it must have been Brian Tuffnel again – had just thrown a lighted stick of the high explosive into this confined place. Foss could see from his present vantage that the fire was almost down to its tamping, and he realized that he would be blown inside out if caught by the trapped forces of the explosions that was now imminent.

His mind raced. To jump down on the stick of dynamite and try to pluck out the stub of its fuse was not to be contemplated. It was too late for that. His only hope lay in passing through the exit before him. If the door should prove to be locked, he could shortly be collecting his shovel to go on duty with the stokers down below, but if he could once put himself on the other side of the door all should be well. One stick of dynamite should do no more than wreck the cellar's interior and ought to leave the house above undamaged.

Foss twisted at the doorknob before him and pulled hard. The door opened, and he sprang through it, jerking the woodwork shut again in his wake; and the exit was no sooner shut once more than a thudding detonation occurred in the root cellar and the basement in which Foss now found himself shook a little and particles of whitewash came fluttering down from the ceiling. Whistling his relief, the foreman lurched across the floor — dodging some pieces of old furniture and other junk in store — clambered up three steps, and opened a door into the corridor beyond. His emergence into the narrow space brought him into almost immediate contact with Mrs Kildare and Brian Tuffnel, who were running towards him from what he knew to be the direction of the hall. 'What was that?' the woman demanded, catching the slightly dazed Foss by the arms and shaking him. 'What are you doing here?'

'Coming up from the root cellar, ma'am,' Foss answered. 'As for the rest of it, I suspect you'd better ask Tuffnel there!'

'What the dickens are you running on about, man?' Tuffnel countered, his elegant pomade adding to the incongruous appearance of the face that carried his bruised eye and bent nose. 'You seem constantly to blame for something these days, Foss!'

'Keep surviving, don't I?' the foreman taunted bitterly. 'If you didn't throw that stick of dynamite into the root cellar just now, there's no man living who did!'

'How so?' Tuffnel asked indigantly. 'I was in the

hall speaking with Mrs Kildare, when the bang occurred!'

'That's correct,' the woman agreed crisply, shoving past the foreman and entering the basement.

Foss craned after her, briefly glimpsing her zig zag movement across the floor at his back and then hearing her open the root cellar door where his gaze could not reach. After that he heard her cry of anger and disgust, and a moment or two later he smelled the raw, sour stench of the exploded dynamite wafting into the house on the draught from the garden.

Mrs Kildare's footsteps sounded again. Her return to the corridor was a quick one. 'It is absolute ruin down there!' she declared, looking up into the foreman's face with accusing eyes.

'What was it before?' Foss inquired grimly. 'I don't know what the devil's going on – but I'll swear you do!'

'I'm sure there'll be no peace around here, Ben Foss,' the woman declared, 'until we've seen the back of you! You'd have been off this ranch hours ago if I'd had my way. Don't take advantage because my daughter seems to favour you!'

'I wouldn't dream of it!' Foss retorted. 'But I'm fed up with these attempts to murder me and folk treating me as if I have the intelligence of a gnat. You're covering up for Tuffnel, Mrs Kildare. He threw that stick of dynamite into the cellar in an attempt to blow me to Kingdom Come. Ma'am, he's in and out of your windows and doors like Springheeled Jack!'

'Brian and I were together in the hall when the explosion took place,' Mrs Kildare said angrily. 'We'd been talking for some minutes. Won't you take my word for anything?'

'Not when I know you're telling a pack of damned lies!' Foss threw back.

'Lies is it now!' Rita Kildare almost shrieked. 'If only my husband were still alive! He'd have tossed you off this property neck-and-crop for how –!'

Feet stamped their approach from the end of the corridor on Foss's right, and Helen Kildare came striding down the passage with the darkest of frowns on her face. 'I thought I could hear you two quarrelling again!' she cried. 'What's it all about this time?'

'It's Ben Foss!' Mrs Kildare declared. 'He was accusing Brian of trying to kill him by throwing a stick of dynamite down on him while he was in the root cellar just now. I've been refuting what he said. Brian was in the hall talking with me when the bang occurred. Your foreman has had the cheek to call me a liar! Now will you fire him?'

'What were you doing in the root cellar, Ben?' Helen asked. 'That place hasn't been opened in a dog's life!'

'Well, that's where your ghost came from last night,' Foss informed her. 'I found proof enough out in the garden that he went down there after I'd chased him round the end of the house. He did his hiding in that hole, and was assisted by Brian Tuffnel when necessary.'

'What have you to say about that, Brian?' Helen Kildare inquired.

'What can I say?' Tuffnel asked disdainfully. 'This is the worst farrago of nonsense that I've ever heard. Yours is the last word, Helen – and this is strictly none of my business – but I'd stand by your mother in this and get rid of that appalling man.'

Helen transfixed Foss with a steely glance, and then she hooked a finger at him. 'This way!' she ordered, her voice damning.

Raising his hands in what amounted to a gesture of amazed defeat, Foss turned and walked after the girl as she headed for the hall. He could not believe this. After all that had occurred – and the number of times that he had already proved to be right – he actually felt that Helen was about to discharge him. Well, that might be for the best. He'd had more than enough of this nonsense! It would be a treat to go somewhere ordinary and just put in a normal day's work. The Circle K had become altogether too rich for his blood, and the foreman's pay didn't cover the kind of misery which had been his of late.

Quietly preparing himself to meet whatever harsh words Helen might soon deliver, Foss followed the girl across the hall and into the room where Brian Tuffnel usually worked – the ranch office that Joe Kildare had furnished long ago – and Helen ordered him to shut the door behind him and then pull up a chair beside the desk. 'Sorry,' she said, smiling as she seated herself in the confidential clerk's chair and pushed a hand into the pocket at the front of her skirt. 'I had to make it sound good back there.'

'Sounded all right to me,' Foss acknowledged dryly, obeying her wishes for his comfort and lowering himself onto a straightbacked chair at the end of the desk on the girl's left. 'So where do we go from here? We seem to keep coming back to this point. Either you believe me or you don't.'

'I believe you,' Helen said. 'I don't even think there's anything much about which you could be mistaken now.' She drew the hand out of the pocket at the front of her skirt and revealed that she was holding an old photograph. Raising it before her, she sat looking at it for a moment or two, then went on: 'Something kept pricking at my memory, Ben. I had to go through dad's personal papers after his funeral, and I had the feeling that I'd seen something among them that might have a bearing on what's been happening in my life this last day or two.' Now, turning in her chair, she held out the photograph to Foss and concluded: 'Please have a good look at that, Ben, and then tell me what you think.'

Foss held the photograph at the level of his breastbone. It was a poor thing – initially blurred and now also faded – and had undoubtedly been taken back in the early eighteen-fifties, when the original daguerreotypes had still to be much improved upon, but two teenage boys were visible in the picture, and their faces were recognizable as those of twins. 'It's your father as a kid,' Foss commented. 'Looks like he had a twin brother. We don't need to look much further for our ghost now, do we?'

'It *appears* not,' the girl stressed. 'Yet never in

my life did I hear dad or anybody else mention that he was one of twins. I just can't understand that, Ben. It seems only to compound – or even confound – one mystery with another.'

'Yeah – well,' Foss drawled, lines notching an inverted V into his forehead above the bridge of his nose. 'Families, y'know, Helen. Queer cattle.'

'I know,' she agreed, shaking her head. 'But I've had more time to think about this than you have, and I sense an actual conspiracy of silence. It's virtually impossible to drop a member from any family without one.'

'I guess you're right,' Foss admitted. 'But we do have to bear in mind that we're going back apiece in this case. Way over a generation. Mayhap a generation and a half.'

'Time for all memory to die,' Helen acknowledged. 'Yet even so – Ben, I'm in my middle twenties. I'm old enough to have heard something.' She paused, clearly waiting for him to comment and, when he didn't, added: 'I suppose there's nothing for it but to ask mother.'

'She'll then know how much we know,' Foss said uncertainly. 'Nice to have an ace-in-the-hole.'

'Or it could shake her up,' Helen observed. 'I don't believe she can have known that photograph still exists. Oh, I wish I could anticipate her reaction.'

'At that,' Foss suddenly allowed, 'it could prove best to ask her and see what happens. This business needs to be encouraged to run on as it will.'

'I guess so.'

'But, Helen.'

'What?'

'With the game – whatever it is – getting shaky,' Foss said judiciously, 'that ghost is bound to turn up again tonight. Likely with a vicious intent. See what I'm driving at?'

'I could come to bodily harm – in my bedroom?'

'Yes. I think this has got past just scaring the wits out of you now.'

'I can't believe my mother would ever let me come to real harm, Ben,' the girl protested – though feebly, and with doubt clouding her gaze.

'She's not the only one in this,' Foss reminded. 'The whole thing could be taken out of her hands. The real enemy could decide that – '

'I've got to die?'

'That would leave *all* paths clear,' Foss stressed. 'No good kidding ourselves, Helen. We've got to look upon the worst that may be there, then make our plans accordingly.'

'This is dreadful, Ben,' the girl breathed. 'I feel sick with fright.'

'Yet it seems to me we have the advantage at the minute,' Foss said reassuringly. 'I know what to do about this – if you'll agree.'

'I'll agree to anything that will keep me alive.'

'Okay, Helen,' he said. 'Here's how it goes. I'm about to leave the house. We've had a big row, and you've fired me. With me gone, your mama should be in just the right mood to be tackled about this photograph.' He tossed the picture back in front of her on the desk. 'You can tell me how that turns out later.'

'What later?'

'Up in your room – where I aim to hide under the bed,' Foss explained grimly. 'I'll be lying in wait to come out at the right moment and give that ghost a bigger scare than he's ever given you.'

'Very well,' the girl said, her features appearing wooden, most likely to hide all manner of unspoken objections. 'But how are you going to reach my bedroom unseen. Everything must depend on that being achieved in secrecy.'

'Simple,' Foss replied. 'I shall ride down the meadow to that stand of trees which grows near the stream. I'll tie my horse into the undergrowth – where nobody is likely to see it – then sneak back up here. I'll enter the house through the root cellar, and creep upstairs when I see my chance.'

'If you keep moving to the left on leaving the basement,' the girl said, after giving her chin a jerk of approval, 'you'll turn a corner and come to the backstairs. You'll then be able to climb to the landing with almost no risk of being seen.'

'Got you.'

She gave him a broad wink. Then, standing up abruptly, she slammed her hands down on the desktop and shouted: 'Get out of here, Ben Foss! You're an ungrateful wretch and a thoroughly low man! I pray to heaven that I may never see your face again, and please don't ever apply to me for a reference! Your behaviour towards my mother has been a disgrace! I'll never forgive it!'

'Ouch!' Foss whispered, grinning in wry amusement as he left his chair and made for the door. Then, turning the knob and moving out into the hall, he raised his own voice a little and snarled back: 'I've had enough of your ranch, Miss Kildare! It's no place for a man to work. I'm off – and to hell with you!'

Acting in high dudgeon, Foss strode along the hall in the direction of the back door. He passed Mrs Kildare and Brian Tuffnel on the way. They spoke no word, but gazed at him triumphantly.

SEVEN

Though he needed food, Foss by-passed the cookhouse, realizing that no genuinely discharged man would take a now unauthorized meal from his former employer or go among his previous workmates offering explanations of what had occurred; so he simply untied his horse from the corral rail to which it was attached and mounted up, riding eastwards around the northern end of the house, and then, as the falling land carried him out of sight of the dwelling, drifted southwards across the grass, bringing the home stream, the Kildare burial ground, and the stand of timber which he sought into view.

As he passed the black iron railings which enclosed the still newish mound of the late Joe Kildare's grave, Foss noted that nothing had been disturbed since he was last this way and that fresh flowers filled the stone vases at the dead man's head and feet. There, he felt sure, Joe would lie quiet until the Last Trumpet should sound, and he wondered uneasily where the man playing the deceased rancher's ghost was hiding at present – since the hellion could hardly be far

away, and there was a definite risk that the twin
whom he believed to be responsible for the
haunting up yonder could be watching him right
now; but there were latent risks in every danger-
ous situation, and he had to accept that this was
just another that went with the present one.

He came to the timber. This, mingling
cottonwoods, pussywillow and birch, smelled
green and full of sap. Dismounting, he led his
horse into the cool shadows of the low-hanging
foliage and tied it where the grass was thick
underfoot and encircling bushes would screen it
from all but the closely visiting eye. Then he
slowly hunkered down and had him a think, since
he wondered whether he could improve on the
course of action which he had recently outlined to
Helen, but he eventually decided that what he
had suggested did indeed cover the main
probabilities best and that he would change
nothing already intended.

Rising, he made his way back to the edge of the
little wood and peered out. Off to his left cows
were grazing, and on his right a flock of birds was
feeding in the waterside grass. But there was no
human activity visible in the neighbourhood, and
Foss reckoned that he had the area to himself in
all that mattered. Then, hitching his gunbelt and
deriving what cover he could from the slight
bumps and terraces of this roughly ascending
corner of the Kildare range, Foss climbed back in
the direction of the ranch house, praying that
Brian Tuffnel had now returned to work in the
office and that no eye, either casual or suspicious,

was presently looking out of a window at the dwelling's front.

Nearing the foot of the front garden, Foss knelt into a small hollow and studied both the bedroom windows and those of the library and drawing room below. No movement took place behind any piece of glass, and he made up his mind to get this over quickly. So, keeping low, he zig zagged a course towards the twin lilac trees that grew near the entrance to the root cellar and entered the shade of the one on the right before pausing again.

The way into the underground room was still open. Once more darting furtively, Foss brought himself to the head of the cellar steps and hurried downwards into the dark again. The reek of high explosives was still present in the subterranean chamber, but the fumes themselves seemed to have cleared away and, moving his feet carefully now for fear that there might be fallen masonry around – which wasn't in fact the case – Foss passed across the cellar floor and located the inner stair, groping his way up it after that.

Next he entered the basement; and then he tiptoed across it and stepped out into the corridor beyond. Turning left now, as Helen had suggested, he rounded the corner of which she had spoken and came to the backstairs. These he climbed as quietly as he could, and reached the passage above which connected the steps with the main landing about half a minute later. It was easy after that to slip past the door of the room adjoining Helen's and then enter the short corridor which provided an approach to the girl's sleeping place.

Foss gave no warning of his presence – for he realized that even a light knock on woodwork could carry far in the silence of the house – and he eased open Helen's door and quickly slipped into the bedroom itself. The girl was there, probably waiting for him, and she sat looking in the glass of her dresser as he catfooted across the floor towards her. She began to rise, but obeyed his reflected signal to stay seated, then looked round and up at him. 'Thank God you've got here,' she said. 'Did you have any difficulties?'

'None,' he responded, shaking his head. 'What did your mother say?'

'It was all very interesting,' Helen confided – 'but not very helpful.'

'Did she deny that your father was one of twins?' Foss asked in surprise.

'No,' Helen answered. 'She told me the story with no more than the reluctance you'd expect in the circumstances.'

'Tell me.'

'There was a twin, and his name was Jacob. Jacob was no good; never was – right from the start. He got into all kinds of trouble as a small boy, and literally disgraced himself by stealing from the other boys when he and dad were sent to school back East. His doings harmed his brother almost as much as himself, and the pair of them had to be withdrawn from the academy in which they had been placed.' Helen paused to gesture the inevitability of it all. 'It got worse as the twins grew older. There were more thefts, and a killing; but Jake had grown crafty by this time and managed to evade all blame. Then, during the war, as an officer in the Federal army, he took to heavy gambling. His luck was poor, and money passed through his hands like water. My grandfather kept paying his debts – as much for the honour of the family as anything else – but it couldn't go on, of course, and the poor old man had to draw a line.' The girl grimaced at her own image in the glass. 'Jake hadn't got the sense to take the hint and mend his ways. No, he went on as before and found himself in real straits. Owing thousands, he, as the regimental treasurer – about the worst job any-body could have trusted him with – stole the money in his keeping and gambled it all away in an effort to make enough to pay off his creditors. I have no doubt he would have been arrested and charged with theft in due course, but his regiment was ordered south before that could happen. It seems – Well, from what mother told me –'

'Go on,' Foss urged.

'From what Jake told my father – just before he entrained in Washington for the journey down into Virginia – he believed his one path of escape was to desert to the enemy. There seems a fair certainty he would have done that –'

'But?'

'His train – which was also pulling two or three cars of ammunition – unexpectedly came under Rebel artillery fire. The train was hit by a shell and the ammunition blew up. Almost all the soldiers on that train were killed; but Jake had been the officer placed in charge of the ammunition cars, and his station aboard was much closer to the main explosion than that of anybody else.'

'He was blown to bits?' Foss prompted impatiently.

'Almost, Ben,' the girl returned. 'They found his greatcoat and about enough of him left to bury; and, when it was all over – and the family had been told all – grandfather said it had been bad enough that Jake had been a thief and a killer, but that he had been a potential traitor also was the worst possible thing. Jake was beyond forgiveness, and grandfather ordered that his name be struck from the family Bible and never spoken in the house again. And it never has been.'

'Until today,' Foss mused. 'What you're saying, Helen, is that your father's twin has been dead for more than twenty years and can't be the living man that I know to be our ghost.'

'Yes, that's what I'm saying,' she admitted.

'So you believe what your mother told you?' Foss sighed.

'She – she seemed convinced of it all herself,' Helen said hesitantly.

'Well, I'm not convinced,' Foss commented bluntly. 'Your Uncle Jake's story may be true up to the point of the train blowing up, but I'd almost stake my own life that he survived that explosion and seized his chance to drop from sight. This is a huge country, Helen. He could've slunk off anywhere once he'd got clear of the wreckage.' He gave a short, disdainful laugh. 'Your mother couldn't confess to you that Jake was still alive without admitting herself guilty of letting your uncle terrorize you. Now isn't that right?'

'I don't know what's exactly right,' Helen breathed at him hotly. 'You're a man who deals in black and white, Ben. There can be shades of guilt. If mother has wronged me in some way, I'm sure there's what she believes to be a good reason for it.'

'Good reason!' Foss protested, finding it difficult to keep his voice down. 'There couldn't possibly be a good reason for anything like that!'

'Don't get het up,' Helen soothed. 'This could still be a long day.'

'Sure,' he agreed soberly. 'Little could still go as I expect. When did it ever anyhow? I've fathomed how the ghost got into the house for his first visit to your room – almost certainly coming up the backstair that I just used – but I've never been wholly sure of what actually happened in here. I got the impression our haunter suddenly appeared to you. One moment he wasn't there, sort of, and the next he was. Is that how it seemed?'

'Yes,' the girl responded.

'He didn't simply come in through the door?'

'N – no.'

'Fact is,' Foss grumbled, 'you're not sure. I figure you were so badly scared your brain froze up.'

'I'd had *two* bad frights about then,' Helen insisted. 'First I saw him down in the yard – which I think stunned me – and then I found him in this room with me – which I know caused me to faint right off.'

'I wish I wasn't so dad-blasted confused by that

bit,' Foss said through his teeth. 'But you can only
go back to how it was then, of course.'

'If he shows up tonight, Ben, none of that will
matter.'

'That's the cure-all,' Foss acknowledged.

Helen rose from her seat at the dresser. 'I can't
spend the rest of the day up here, Ben.'

'That would be crazy!' he agreed. 'Off you go
downstairs. Do your normal things.'

'You'll just have to stick it out.'

'I expected that.'

'You can doze.'

'I can sleep too.'

'Anything I can do for you, Ben?'

He rubbed a hand over his empty stomach. 'I
could sure do with some grub, Helen.'

'Hungry again,' she chided.

'I haven't eaten since Adam was a pup!' Foss
protested. 'It's been non-stop.'

'I'll sneak some food up to you,' Helen promised,
moving past him to the door – 'when I can.'

He nodded, and she went out. Then, sitting
down on the side of the girl's bed, he listened to
her descent into the lower house and heard her
strike up a conversation with her mother in the
kitchen, though he could distinguish no word of
what was being said. The talk muttered on for a
minute or two, then the house seemed to settle
into complete silence and, easing off his boots,
Foss raised his feet from the floor and stretched
out his body upon the bed. Closing his eyes, he
made his mind largely blank and tried to rest, and
he was hovering somewhere between sleep and

waking, when it seemed to him that he heard a dull yet ponderous movement from the wall on his left.

Abruptly coming fully awake, he sat up quietly and turned an uncertain frown towards the adjoining room, his gaze then settling on the door of the closet which he had looked into after Helen's fright the night before. In some curious way, the noise that he had just heard had seemed to originate from that cupboard. Could there be somebody hiding in there? Was he due for a supernatural visitation in broad daylight? Turning his legs off the coverlet, he stood up and drew his revolver, then padded round the foot of the bed in his stockinged feet, making for the closet. He was determined to give anybody who might be hiding there a real bad shock; but, on jerking open the door and looking inside the cupboard, he saw neither more nor less than he had seen before – a lot of emptiness, a little dust, and the rows of pegs on which clothing could be hung.

Putting up his gun, he allowed himself a rather twisted grin over his mistake. Then he thrust out a fist and gave the rear wall of the closet a little knock to give him some idea of how solid it was. It seemed not too thickly built at all and even to yield a trifle under the force employed. Frowning again, Foss flattened his palm against what he imagined to be painted brickwork and struck once more – using greater strength this time – and he heard a metallic click and the entire back of the cupboard swung away from him to the left, revealing that it was in fact a concealed door.

Stepping into the closet, Foss peered through the space which he had opened up. He saw a room before him that had the neglected appearance of one that had not been in use for a long time. This room was furnished in pieces of massive oak. It had a heavy bed standing with its head against the wall on the right, and upon this bed an ageing man of considerable inches lay asleep and snoring softly. Despite himself and what he now knew, the hair again prickled on Foss's nape, for he might have been gazing upon his late employer's resurrected form. Yet the sleeper, regardless of doubling Joe Kildare, had a wicked face that even in repose suggested a devilish snarl. There beyond any shadow of doubt lay Jacob Kildare, and no further proof was needed that he had survived the explosion which others believed had blown him to pieces over twenty years ago.

Hand resting on the butt of his gun, Foss pondered what he ought to do next, while sniffing at the stagnant air which had started to percolate from the second bedroom. The atmosphere carried a taint that was not unlike that from smouldering brown paper, and his attention was drawn to a small table that stood beside the head of the bed. Upon the table lay a plate, and on the plate rested a wooden pipe and three small balls of a greyish-brown substance. Opium. Foss had seen it often enough in the dens about the larger western towns. So Jake Kildare was an opium smoker. Well, that accounted for the depth of his present sleep. Any normal sleeper – in that man's tense situation – would have awakened at the first

knock on the wall and been up and ready at the
opening of the concealed door. Foss might well
have stopped a bullet before he could do anything
about it. But he judged that just now Mrs
Kildare's secret guest was drugged to the extent
that he would not waken short of having cold
water thrown over him.

About then Foss heard movement in the room
at his back. Craning, he saw that Helen had just
slipped in with a plate of sandwiches in her hand.
Coming to an abrupt halt, she stood peering
towards the closet in dawning bewilderment; and,
retreating from the threshold of the second room,
Foss beckoned to her and whispered: 'Put the
sandwiches down, Helen, and come here. I want
you to see what I've found. Only don't faint on me
– because this is going to be a great shock.'

The girl set the plate of sandwiches down on the
dresser. After that she stepped over to the closet.
Foss moved aside and let her pass into the
cupboard's interior. Then he padded up in her
wake and gripped her upper arms with supportive
hands. 'Great heavens alive!' she breathed,
jibbing in horrified amazement as she gazed
through the opening before her at the occupant of
the bed beyond. 'Can I believe what I'm seeing?'

'You can,' Foss hissed in her ear. 'There's some
more proof of your mother's guilt. Who else can
that be but Jake Kildare?'

'Nobody.'

'Still afraid of ghosts?'

'Please, Ben.'

'Just funning.'

'Don't mock me.'

'How if I hug you?'

'Fine,' Helen said – 'but not right now.'

He sensed her need to withdraw. Retreating himself, he steered her out of the closet after him. Then, after he had released her and she had seated herself on the edge of the bed adjacent, he re-entered the cupboard and shut the secret door. Finally, he backed out again and closed the closet door also. 'What is it to be, Helen?' he asked softly. 'You're the boss. More so than usual in this. This is your family, and the folk we have to do with are your relations. You're going to have to live with whatever action you take here.'

'I feel like sending for the sheriff,' Helen said bitterly. 'But my own! Can you see any other way?'

'Not that wouldn't leave the hellions free to plot against you again,' Foss answered.

The door behind them let out a faint squeak. They both craned quickly, and Foss saw that Mrs Kildare had crept into the room while they were speaking. The older woman's eyes first widened and then blazed with fury, and she lunged across the bed and seized her daughter, kneeling herself on the coverlet as she shook Helen violently. 'Hussy!' she cried. 'I knew you were up to something you shouldn't be! Fancy allowing that man into your bedroom! How far has this gone? Have I anything to worry about?'

'Mrs Kildare,' Foss answered grimly, 'you've got plenty to worry about. But not what you suppose.'

'We know who's in the next room, mother,'

Helen said shortly. 'I suppose you had that secret connecting door built while I was away at the Cattlemen's Convention in Cheyenne a month or two ago? How long ago was this wickedness planned? What is it you're seeking, mother? My death?'

'That's too absurd, Helen!' Mrs Kildare announced defiantly. 'How did you find out about –?'

'Jake?' Foss queried. 'He's full of opium and fit to sleep for hours. It was real quiet in here. I reckon I heard the big polecat roll over in bed. The rest just followed naturally.'

'Men!' the woman railed.

'Get in the way somewhat, don't we?' Foss agreed ironically. 'Yet it mostly takes female kind to get really wicked. Your daughter asked you a question, ma'am. You haven't answered her.'

'I did.'

'No, you didn't,' Foss contradicted. 'Perhaps you need me to refresh your memory. What is it you're seeking, Mrs Kildare?'

'Nothing,' Rita Kildare said, sliding backwards off the bed and slapping her thighs. 'Nothing – nothing – nothing!'

'Too many nothings,' Foss said. 'They must add up to a heap.'

'Mother,' Helen said, 'this is cards on the table time. You have been found out, and you are not in charge of this situation. You are in fact our prisoner. I want you to tell me exactly what's been going on. If you don't, I'll have the sheriff called in from Foxpark and a proper investigation made.

I'm pretty sure that will end with Uncle Jake and you being locked up in the cells.'

'You – you can't talk to me like – like that!' Mrs Kildare spluttered.

'I just did, mother,' Helen said flatly. 'We all accept that self-preservation is the first law of Nature. I feel myself to be seriously threatened, and I intend to protect myself by every means I can.' She paused to allow what she had said to sink in. 'I'm giving you a chance. But all ties of blood and family are in abeyance right now. Will you co-operate?'

'What a wicked and ungrateful girl you are!' Mrs Kildare protested, eyes blinking wetly as she made an abrupt change of tack. 'Have you no feelings?'

'Spare us the tears and reproaches, ma'am,' Foss advised. 'If your daughter weakens, I won't.'

'You're two of a kind, Ben Foss!'

'Sure,' Foss acknowledged dryly. 'Me and Helen are a pair of right nice folk on the quiet – and you're playing us for fools. Won't do, ma'am; we see through you. Now get to it – or else!'

Once more there was an unexpected movement at the bedroom door, and this time it was Brian Tuffnel who entered. The confidential clerk held a cocked revolver in his right hand. 'I feared you were in trouble,' he said, glancing quickly at Rita Kildare.

'Yes, boy,' the woman said. 'I'm afraid things have come unstuck. Keep them covered while I take Ben Foss's gun.'

'Yes, mother,' the young man said.

Foss felt his jaw drop. Now that one did come as a surprise.

EIGHT

Foss quickly switched his gaze to Helen. He perceived that she too was amazed. Then, as if convinced that what Tuffnel had just said could not be the literal truth, she snapped: 'What nonsense are you encouraging now, mother? I know you've always wanted a son – and have often treated Brian Tuffnel like one – but I think you'd better stop playing "let's pretend" before you come to believe that what you're pretending is the truth.'

'He is my son, Helen,' Rita Kildare said shortly, removing Foss's revolver from its holster and then stepping well back with the heavy weapon clasped between both hands. 'He's your half-brother, and Jake Kildare is his father.'

'So that's why dad chose me to be his heir!' Helen exclaimed, studying Tuffnel in a manner that told he found no favour in her eye. 'Dad knew about – about him and – and was afraid that you'd bring him here as the new master if he left the ranch to you. It strikes me he must have known Uncle Jake was still alive too.'

'No, he didn't know that,' Mrs Kildare said.

112

'Only I knew that. Jake's misdeeds had been so terrible that he dared not even let his twin brother know that he had survived the blowing up of his southbound train by that Rebel artillery.'

'How did he come to survive?' Foss inquired curiously.

Mrs Kildare shrugged, as if saying that it could hardly matter what he and her daughter knew now. 'The irony of chance,' she explained. 'Jake had for some reasons stepped up to ride with the engineer, after the locomotive had watered on the other side of the Potomac, and another man back with the ammunition cars must have put on Jake's greatcoat by mistake. Anyway, Jake was unharmed when the high explosives went up and, realizing how few the survivors were, took his opportunity to desert – without having any idea as to the true extent of his good fortune. And it was only later, when the story of the train and a detailed casualty list were published, that he realized his old identity had been dissolved forever and that he could now live confidently in the new one that he had already given himself. He rode west, to San Francisco, and lived out the years as they came – looking for his chance.'

'Which he's now got here,' Foss gritted. 'I never have liked you much, Rita Kildare – and I like you a heck of a lot less this minute – but if I were you, I'd see that dopehead through there out of my life before he ruined it entirely.'

'I know now why mother used to go alone on holiday to the West Coast when she was younger,' Helen said bitterly. 'Dad provided the means, but it was clearly the wicked brother that she loved and yearned for.'

'A woman can love two men,' Rita Kildare retorted. 'Your father had all that he wanted of me, and he was aware that I'd already had a son by his brother when he married me. His only stipulation was that I put the past firmly behind me and Jake's child out to adoption. I pretended to do what he wished; but I had some money of my own and arranged to have Brian live with foster parents. I was even able to give him a gentleman's education when the time came. You see the results before you.'

'What I see is a man plainly intent on displacing your daughter,' Foss said. 'He's another Jake Kildare in the making. You've nothing to be very proud of, woman!'

'Be careful how you speak to my mother!' Tuffnel snarled, loosing a backhander that split the foreman's lips and sent him reeling. 'The hands all know by now that you were fired today and ordered off the Circle K in disgrace. If you were to disappear this afternoon, it's my belief that no questions would be asked in the territory concerning you. You're alone in the world, are you not?'

Foss made no answer. Tuffnel had got his facts right and summed up the matter exactly. Foss was the last of his line – a remarkably undistinguished one – and, if he vanished from the earth today, nobody would care a jot. That made him realize that he must watch points and try to keep alive. Only dead was dead. He might get out of this yet.

Mrs Kildare said: 'We can't stand around like

this indefinitely, Brian. This ranch doesn't run itself. Somebody is sure to come looking for one of us before long. You'll have to go into the next room and awaken your father. I think we should make that room a prison for now.'

'You go and wake him up,' Tuffnel urged. 'Let me watch these two. Foss is a crafty man – none more so – and you might find it difficult to kill him if he got up to his tricks.'

'I would not,' Rita Kildare said, a note of pure hatred in her voice – 'but it might indeed be wiser if I roused that foolish man from his present state. Very well; I'll go.'

The woman walked up to the closet. Foss watched her open it and step inside. Now she pushed back the secret door and again revealed the room beyond. The sleeper was lying upon his oaken bed in the same position as before. Rita Kildare moved out into the second room. She rounded the foot of the bed and went up to the washstand on its further side. Here she took the towel from the stand's rail and soaked it in the water jug. After that she stepped up to the head of the bed and threw the sheet and blankets off the drugged man, who was naked except for a pair of long drawers. Then she gave him a good shaking – which caused him to growl and grumble in his sleep – and suddenly placed the sodden towel on his bared diaphragm.

The man on the bed jerked convulsively, then struck out blindly with his right fist; but Mrs Kildare, clearly ready for something of the sort, stepped back and dodged the ponderous blow –

snatching the towel off Jake's midriff a moment
later and squeezing out much of the cold water
that soaked it upon his face. This caused the big
man to spit, splutter, swear, and then sit up, both
hands wiping at his wet features. 'Damn you,
Rita!' he snarled, his worn brown teeth dripping a
foul saliva and his opaque eyes, with their
yellowed whites, glaring dangerously. 'What's up
with you? Are you trying to drown me? You knew
I'd be trying to get a few hours sleep. It could be a
busy night again.'

'Possibly,' the woman agreed coldly. 'But not
quite as you expect.'

'Why?' Jake asked thickly. 'What's happened?'

'If you weren't full of opium,' Rita accused,
'you'd have found out before now. Ben Foss and
my girl know about the secret door, you, and more
or less everything else.'

'Ben Foss? That long-shanked foreman? I
thought you told me he'd been sent packing?'

'Helen deceived me over that,' the woman
explained. 'But it's all right. Brian is holding
Helen and Ben prisoner in the next room.'

'By the Lord Harry!' Jake raged disgustedly,
turning himself off the bed and standing dazedly
as he picked up and fumbled on the clothing that
he must earlier have kicked off beside it. 'Can I
rely on nobody to do anything properly?'

'Everything has been done properly,' Mrs
Kildare retorted. 'You haven't changed one bit
across the years. You made too little allowance for
the brains of others. Ben Foss is sharp, and my
daughter is no fool either.'

'Pah!' Jake sneered at her. 'I've never gone in for sublety, Rita. It was you who insisted on all that fiddle-faddle of the ghost and such. If you want somebody out of the way, put them out of the way – permanently!'

'That girl is my daughter, Jake!' Rita Kildare protested, a hint of warning in her tones. 'I won't kill one child in order to give another more than he was born to. And I won't seal my foolish love for a bad man in blood. How I wish I'd never allowed myself to be talked into any of this. I'm sure Helen would have made good provision for you two if I'd been open about it. After all, Joe Kildare is gone and nothing can hurt him any more. What we're doing now is wrong – wrong – and then a thousand times wrong!'

'Heigh-ho!' Jake jeered, going to the washstand, picking up the ewer, and drinking from it in great thirsty gulps. 'Listen to her run on! If it's gone wrong, it's gone wrong, and it's no good kicking against the pricks, my honey! You're in this with Brian and me – right up to your sweet neck! There's no room for restraint any more, Rita! Whatever must be done to win the day for us, will have to be done, and that's all there is to it! Even if it comes to murder!'

'God help us, Jake!' Mrs Kildare responded, shuddering visibly.

'If there'd been a God,' Jake chewed, 'He'd never have made this world in the first place! Don't worry about God, my woman! The laws men make are all you need be afraid of!'

'That's blasphemy, Jake!'

'Where's the thunder and lightning?' the big man asked, stalking round the foot of the bed and heading for the way into the adjoining room.

Foss watched with a critical eye as Jake Kildare stepped through the secret door and entered Helen's bedroom. The light from the windows was still good and, in peering at the evil-looking Jake from close range, Foss could detect at least two big differences between the late Joe and the Kildare twin still extant. Jake was stooped – something his brother had never been – and the seamed and flaking skin of Jake's smudging features betrayed a life of many excesses lived away from the sun. Joe, with his outdoor tan and dignity of feature, had looked the world right in the eye and suffered no diminution of presence right up to the end; but Jake had lost all trace of a superior being's natural authority and developed the sly, veiled look of a low fellow. Born of the same mother the two might have been, but whereas Joe had reached his full potential as a human being, Jake had clearly undergone a spiritual degeneration from which there was no return. Foss, who had revered old Joe, felt nothing but contempt for the man here who looked so like him and yet was so unalike.

But Jake Kildare clearly had little interest in Foss and less in what he thought. The big man's attention was centred on Helen, and his face took on an amused leer as the girl shrank away from him. Raising his hands, he pounced at her, making a weird hooting noise, and she cried out in fright and backed right up against the wall.

'Stop that nonsense, Jake!' Rita Kildare ordered. 'We're past such childish behaviour!'

'Are we?' Jake inquired, letting out a sinister laugh. 'Ask your girl!'

'Get through there, Helen!' Mrs Kildare ordered. 'You go with her, Ben.'

Nodding, Foss moved across the room and, catching the girl in the crook of his left arm, steered her back through the secret door and into the room where Jake had been sleeping. Pulling up a chair, he sat the quivering Helen down — patting her on the shoulder to make her aware that he understood how she felt — and then he seated himself on the side of the bed and looked into the other room, where Rita Kildare was making small gestures and whispering animatedly to Jake and Brian Tuffnel. Then, seeming to have obtained some kind of agreement from the two men, she turned from them and gazed through at the captives. 'Jake and I are going downstairs,' she said. 'Now I tell you this. The door to that room is locked and the window jammed. There's no way out. We are leaving Brian up here to watch you. There will be no trouble if you behave yourselves. Please do that.'

Foss gave his head a jerk, and the woman and Jake Kildare withdrew to begin their descent. They left Tuffnel leaning on Helen's dresser. There was a bored expression on the young man's face as he watched the captives through the secret door. Studying the other's body movements, Foss had the impression that Tuffnel was about to enter the prison room via the closet and join his charges, but in fact the confidential clerk stayed where he was and began to pace up and down. His restlessness increased with each passing minute, and it eventually took him out of the door of Helen's bedroom and into the passage beyond. There he lingered, a hand jingling change in his pocket – a man perhaps too sure of himself and the situation that had been placed in his charge.

It was then, with Tuffnel out of sight and close earshot, that Helen leaned back in her chair and murmured: 'Ben, I know something they don't. The door to this room has a loose upper hinge and will rock back slightly on it. The tongue of the lock is also damaged. It received a heavy blow when we were moving these pieces of oak furniture in here.'

'So?' Foss breathed at her.

A quick backward pace brought Tuffnel back into Helen's bedroom at that instant. He peered through at his prisoners and asked suspiciously: 'Were you talking?'

'What have we got to talk about?' Foss countered shortly. 'You should be able to see your sister is sick at the stomach.'

'My half-sister,' Tuffnel corrected distastefully. 'We don't choose our relations.'

'We most certainly don't!' Helen agreed.

'Be quiet, the pair of you,' Tuffnel ordered – 'and keep still!'

'I've every intention of doing just that,' Foss promised, folding his arms and closing his eyes. 'It isn't often I get the chance of a rest at this time of the day.'

'I think you will soon be in a state of eternal

rest,' Tuffnel taunted, his footfalls starting to vibrate through the floorboards again as he resumed his pacing.

Foss listened and waited. Tension quivered in his scalp and cold sweat bled from his temples. He felt that Helen Kildare had already told him enough, and he meant to act upon her information the next time – if ever – that their captor strayed out into the passage again. Why couldn't this fellow prove reliable in his unreliability? If he would just take himself out towards the landing for a single minute, Foss judged that it ought to be possible for him to leave the bed, cross the room – apply the most silent test he could to the door – and, if necessary, return undetected to his seat again. But Tuffnel refused to oblige; he seemed content to idle to Helen's room since that one brief journey astray.

And so it went on, minute by slow minute, with the silence of the house like a crawling presence and the dead atmosphere like a choking reflection of the hush. Foss's nerves twitched and jumped, his solar plexus screwed tighter and tighter, and his own perspiration began to stink sourly in his nostrils. Still Tuffnel remained in Helen's room, pacing – pacing; and Foss was on the verge of accepting that he was to be given no chance to reach the door – and would almost certainly have found the effort futile if he had – when Rita Kildare's voice echoed up from the hall, inquiring as to whether Brian would like 'a cup of tea and a slice of cake.'

Tuffnel's head came erect, and he acted as

almost anybody might have predicted, moving
quickly out into the passage beyond his half-
sister's room and shouting down an affirmative
reply from the best spot he could reach; and Foss,
coming sharply back to life again – and calming
instantly – reckoned that he had now got the only
chance he was going to get and rose silently from
the edge of the bed, gliding towards the door on
what he suddenly realized were still stockinged
feet.

He reached the woodwork. There was simply no
second to waste. Cupping a hand over the
doorknob, he turned and threw his weight
backwards, pulling strongly as he felt the
woodwork give a little, and the door came open
with an airy shudder but hardly a sound. Despite
Helen's promising words, it seemed quite incredible – even the miracle of the day – and Foss
glanced back towards the girl, grinning comically.
'The sheriff!' she mouthed at him. 'Go for the
sheriff!'

It was a sensible enough command, and Foss
didn't have the time to think around it; so, putting
his head out into the passage beyond him, he
peered to the left – fearing that Tuffnel might
have halted somewhere near the landing and be
in a position to hear any noise he made if not
actually to see him – and it gave him a nasty turn
as he found himself looking at the back of a
Tuffnel who had been standing just a pace or two
from the head of the stairs and only that very
instant swung away from a placement which
would almost certainly have brought him a

glimpse of the prisoner's emerging face. But it had not happened, and a relieved Foss watched as the other passed from sight and his footfalls headed back towards Helen's bedroom.

Foss felt a momentary sense of freedom, yet he knew that his time of grace would probably not last for more than seconds. Much must now depend on Tuffnel's immediate state of concentration or, perhaps, Helen's ability to deceive the man into believing that he, Foss, although no longer sitting on the bed, was still in the room with her. Such a belief could delay Tuffnel's natural reactions for that brief time more. But almost everything thus perceived was in the lap of the gods, and Foss padded out into the corridor before him – greatly assisted at this stage by his lack of boots – and turned right, darting for the backstairs.

Down these he went, descending at a breakneck pace and, judgement fine tuned in this crisis, sprang out over the last four and landed lightly in the passage below. Now he dashed for the way into the basement and, gaining the lowest level of the house itself, crossed to the door of the root cellar. Passing through this, he scampered down into the darkness at the bottom of the vault, able to see that the steps which led up to the garden were still unsealed above – but discovering now the disadvantage of being bootless, for he found himself treading a carpet of debris which seemed all sharp points and tiny cutting edges.

His clean, swift movements of a few moments ago reduced to an ungainly hobble, Foss reached

the stair that gave access to the daylight above
and paused for just the instants necessary to wipe
the clinging fragments off the soles of his cotton
socks. After that he scaled the steps at the speed
which his mind continued to insist upon and rose
once more into the light, his feet suffering new
tortures as he trampled out amidst the young
shoots and other types of spiky growth around the
foot of the lilac tree to his left.

He had no doubt that blood was seeping by now
– and that his misery had only just started – but
the need for speed and more speed smothered his
pain and he went off down the garden like a hare.
With every second he expected to hear an outcry
or a shot in his wake, but he cleared the cultivated
ground without any alarm going up and crouched
into his run, veering off to his right and coming to
the shallow terraces of rough grassland which
settled towards the home stream and the small
wood beside it in which he had left his horse tied
an hour or two ago.

Reaching the foot of the descending land, Foss
craned back and upwards, but there was no sign
of pursuit and he began to get the feeling that he
could still survive this, and he entered the trees
and soon located his mount. Freeing the brute
from where he had tied it, he climbed into his
saddle; then, lying forward on the horse's mane –
the more easily to clear the branches and foliage
that hung in his path – he steered for the edge of
the timber and nudged into the clear at the
moment of reaching it. Then he spurred northwards along the bank of the stream, looking

inwardly towards the place – about two miles ahead – where he could join the trail to Foxpark.

Suddenly a rifle banged high on his left. He heard a bullet rip through a cluster of leaves and then bury itself in the trunk of a nearby tree. He glanced swiftly towards the spot from which the shot had come. There, about three hundred yards away, crouching on a moon-shaped vantage, he made out the big figure of Jake Kildare. The fellow had a Winchester to his shoulder and was again taking aim; but Foss reckoned that his enemy would have to be a far better shot than most to nail him at that range; so he ignored Kildare – and two more quickly levered shots that came his way – and passed his eye round and about, figuring that, in the present circumstances, the younger man – presumably fleet of foot and certainly clever enough to anticipate the direction in which the escaper would head – was the one to fear.

Then he saw Tuffnel before him. The young man had just stepped out from behind a bush growing near the Kildare burial ground. Tuffnel moved to face sideways on. Standing like a duellist, he looked along the sights of his revolver, left arm bent and fist resting on the back of his hip – a daunting sight; and in a frantic effort to unsettle the other, Foss galloped straight at him, yelling blue murder; but Tuffnel kept his nerve and fired. The bullet missed Foss's left temple by perhaps a tenth of an inch, but the flash of the pistol frightened his horse. Checking abruptly, the creature reared almost to the vertical and, taken largely by surprise, Foss lost his grip on his reins and was catapulted backwards out of his seat.

He struck the earth with great violence, and his senses left him in a fiery eruption that almost instantly shrank into darkness.

NINE

Foss recovered his senses very slowly indeed. There was a time, as his inching consciousness first touched the edge of true perception, when everything seemed to become pleasantly warm, soothingly hazy, and filled with threads of luminous colour. A very deep instinct told him that he was either dead or close to death, and that he need only slip back into the restful darkness from which he had so recently emerged and it would all be over and he would never need to strive again for any earthly thing. But there was also another voice present – this one stern and censorious – which warned that he was still young, had done no more than a tithe of what was possible to him as yet, and should not give up on life just because he was a little hurt and it would be so easy to do so at this moment. So he began to make a struggle of it, hanging on to his incipient awareness for all that he was worth, and his effort brought him – pain. Pain in his head, pain in his back and kidneys, pain in his feet – pain everywhere; and he groaned and muttered to himself, realizing that he had been bound hand

and foot as he at last tried to move his limbs.

Again he became still, and he went on suffering; but, while the suffering stayed with him, it did grow more endurable and his perceptions hardened. At first he could not quite grasp where he was, for he had the sky above him – a golden evening sky – but was enclosed by low wooden walls of very limited dimensions; and it took him several minutes to work out that he was lying all trussed up in the bottom of a farm cart that seemed to be standing motionless in a green place that was next to nowhere.

He figured that his enemies must have driven him to some isolated spot on the range – which was perhaps visited only once in months – and there left him to die, and the fact that they had shoved what could have proved to be the tell-tale boots back on his swollen feet seemed to suggest something of that kind. Yet, as his thoughts grew more rational and clear-cut, he gradually perceived that the presence of the cart almost certainly indicated otherwise, since if it had been intended to simply abandon him on the grass to a slow death it was unlikely that a valuable piece of transport would have been left with him. Indeed, it was not even likely that the cart would have been used to carry him to this place at all – for the back of a horse would have done just as well – had his enemies not had some purpose for it that went beyond leaving him in it for the present moment.

About then he felt a small jerk. It was now apparent to him that a horse was between the shafts and grazing. This made him certain that

neither he nor the cart had been abandoned by his
enemies, and the full measure of his relief came
through. Yet it inevitably left him asking himself
what they intended for his immediate future,
since he could not believe that they would let him
stay alive beyond the point that it somehow suited
their plans, and this new apprehension soon
brought back his feelings of weakness and left
him lying limp in body but with his senses
preternaturally taut.

Another hour or so went by. The dusk came and
began to thicken. Foss heard the evening chorus
of the whippoorwills, the hooting of an owl, and
the soft wind blowing through the shadow of the
advancing night. Presently the dusk smothered
the afterglow, but there was still enough light by
which to see as Foss heard the sounds of two
horsemen approaching from the right. Then the
heads of the two horsemen moved into his field of
vision – those of Jake Kildare and Brian Tuffnel –
and the pair halted near the side of the cart and
gazed in upon him. 'I see you've come round, Foss,'
Jake said. 'That was a very bad fall you took –
perhaps the worst I've ever seen. I feared you
might die while we were away.'

'Feared!' Foss echoed. 'How could that be?'

'We may have a use for you yet,' Kildare said
grimly. 'We'll see – we'll see.'

'Not quite, Jake,' Brian Tuffnel said sharply,
addressing the older man as a familiar rather
than the father that he had been declared to be.
'This way or that, it has to be done.'

'It certainly has,' Jake agreed. 'Eschew the

petticoats, lad. I've known many, and they were
all sore trials. Your mother runs about even with
the rest. Though in this matter I can understand
why.'

'We mustn't let that influence us,' Tuffnel said.
'I hope you're not getting soft in your old age.'

'I can still be as hard as you are, Brian,' Jake
Kildare said, chuckling cynically. 'And perhaps
harder. I know all about having the will and
riding roughshod. But the years have taught me
something that you have still to learn. You still
believe you can have anything you want just
because you want it. It may have seemed like that
to you, but it only works so far. Your mother has
been your source, and given you everything you've
asked just for the asking. You think there's no
limit to what you can charm or bully her into. But
there is a limit, and I'm pretty sure you're up
against it now. You talked yourself blue in the
face over dinner, but your mother didn't yield an
inch, did she?'

'If she refuses to give, Jake,' Tuffnel responded,
his expression one of a singular arrogance and
self-assurance, 'we must take.'

'Yes, we must take,' Jake agreed. 'We have no
real choice. That's been apparent for some time.
Yet the price of taking could prove more than we
can afford. There is nothing down on paper that
gives you a blood right to claim on her estate.
Whatever we do ought to be done with her will.
We could lose all by making her hate us.'

'We'll present her with a fait accompli,' Tuffnel
retorted. 'We'll worry later about how she feels

towards us. It may be that you were never a great
success with women because you never really
understood them. With them, love is all. Remove
that and they feel they have nothing left. If we
remove one of the mainstays of mother's life, she
will cling all the tighter to what she has left. We
two. Give it six months and she won't care what
we did to make her mistress of the Circle K.'

'To make you master, young man,' Kildare
corrected. 'I only hope you will prove duly
appreciative.'

'If I prove less,' Tuffnel observed sardonically,
'I'm sure you'll find ways of making me so. But
forget your gambling ways. I won't see money
squandered on that kind of folly!'

'It comes of keeping books and counting
pennies,' Jake sneered. 'You have much of your
grandfather Aaron's tightness in your character,
Brian. Yes, I gambled when I was younger – and I
still do when I have the opportunity – but I'm not
always a loser.'

'Any man who loses more than he wins is a loser
in my estimation,' Tuffnel said coldly. 'But why
are we quarrelling over the details of a future that
we have yet to win? Let's tie these horses to the
back of the cart and take Ben Foss to the place we
decided upon over dinner.'

'Very well,' Jake Kildare said, following his
son's example and dismounting.

The two men led their horses to the back of the
cart and secured them to the tailgate. After that
they walked round to the front of the transport
and climbed onto the driving board. Here they

seated themselves, Kildare ignited a pipeful of tobacco, and Tuffnel picked up the reins and set the horse in motion. They rolled across the darkening range, and it was apparent to the still pain-racked Foss that, judging from where the sun had gone down, they were journeying westwards. Using his imagination, and the dim silhouettes of the surrounding higher ground which sometimes became visible to him, he decided that their starting point had been an expanse of reserve graze about half a mile to the south of the ranch house, and he had the feeling that they were bound in the direction of Signal Hill and possibly the hiding place in which he had come upon Pete Boone. Certainly, even if interested in what had happened to him, nobody would be likely to find him over there. But imagination was not enough; it was all a matter of wait and see.

Presently the prairie moon swung into place and shone out of a clear sky. The silvery light brought a sense of mystery to the whispering grass. Foss smelled Jake Kildare's tobacco and glimpsed the width of the big man's hunched back. Never had he contemplated anybody more of the earth-earthy. It was hard to credit that the shaggy, crumbling villain had lately played the ghost to such good effect; but that only went to prove that fear was entirely of the mind, and that to be frightened folk had to frighten themselves on whatever information came along.

Foss felt an obliquity entering their course. Tuffnel was drawing at his right-hand leather and the cart was moving into a valley of gloom that lay between two shapeless hills. Sure of where they were now, Foss knew himself confirmed in his earlier surmise that the area about Signal Hill was their destination, and before long the vehicle emerged from the gloomy narrows and fetched left into a long, slow turn which brought the occupants of the cart opposite the summit in question and the ridges on its either flank.

The horse kept up its steady pull, and Tuffnel guided it to the right of the hilltop and over the climb there, taking it carefully down the reverse slope with the drag in operation throughout the descent, and they bent sharply north of west on the ground directly behind the ridge and finally drew to a stop at the foot of the slope in which Foss knew the entrance to the old mine that he had himself located yesterday morning to be situated.

Jake Kildare and Brian Tuffnel climbed down from the driving board. One moving on either side, they slouched rather tiredly round to the back of the vehicle. After that Foss heard them free the horses that had been walking in the cart's wake, then pull the pins and lower the tailgate. Next, between them, the two men pulled him into what was roughly a sitting position on the back of the transport and freed his legs – while leaving his upper body independently bound – then set him on his feet. Foss promptly sagged to his knees, and his captors just as quickly yanked him erect once more. Down he went again, and they played their part a second time – Jake

warning him to get a grip on himself or else – and
the greatly weakened Foss would have been
prepared to challenge that threat, but he realized
that he was already hurt enough and could not
stand any more serious maltreatment. Besides, he
had his pride; so he made an enormous effort and
managed to stay upright between his captors.
Jake Kildare left them then and, while Tuffnel
continued to give Foss a little support, walked
over to the two horses standing apart now and
took a lantern off the saddle of one, raising its
chimney and touching off its wick with a match.
Then, with the light adjusted to his satisfaction,
he returned to Foss and Tuffnel and resumed his
position at the prisoner's side. 'Climb,' he snarled
– 'and none of your old buck!'

Foss did his best. Digging his heels in, and
allowing his captors to give him what help they
would, he forced his way slowly up the steep
ascent before him and arrived presently,
breathless and sweating, near the box elder that
screened the mine's adit from below. Now he stood
by while Tuffnel forced back the springy growth
and made room for Jake Kildare to push him
through the opening and then bring him to a stop
at the centre of the cave beyond, the light from the
lantern now an absolute necessity in the
blackness which pressed at them from the inner
earth.

The box elder snapped back into position over
the mouth of the cave as Tuffnel released it behind
him, and Foss was aware of the young man
moving quickly to rejoin Kildare and himself.

After pausing to draw breath, Tuffnel took the lantern from his father's grasp and, holding it before him, ducked into the passage at the cavern's rear. As he did this, it was revealed that he was still holding the rope with which Foss's legs had recently been secured, so it was plain to the prisoner that he could expect to be bound up again and could look forward to a thoroughly uncomfortable night.

They headed deeper into the mine. Tuffnel kept the lantern jiggling slightly at the length of his left arm. Around them dust sifted down, and it helped fill Foss's nostrils with the dry odours of this none too stable excavation. Now they were at the heart of the mine. Here the light of the lantern revealed small reefs of quartz and particles of vestigial silver, signs indicative that a certain amount of precious metal had once been dug out of the rock in this area. Then Tuffnel paused at the mouth of a gallery on his right and shone the lantern into it. 'This will do,' he said. 'We'll put him in here for the night. I'll tie his legs up again.'

'Be sure you make a job of it,' Jake Kildare urged. 'I've never liked leaving bound men by themselves. What a pity we no longer have Boone to rely upon. I gather we have Foss to blame for his death.'

'The debt will be repaid on the morrow,' Tuffnel promised grimly. 'I had no liking for Boone; but he appears to have served you well for a good many years, and that's enough.'

Tuffnel moved aside. Jake Kildare thrust Foss into the mouth of the tunnel exposed. Foss

staggered ahead for about four paces; then,
reaching the gallery's end, sank to the floor and
propped his back against the wall, his two captors
closing on him from behind their light; and
Tuffnel passed the lantern back to his father and
then knelt and tied Foss's ankles together again,
winding the rope around the rest of the prisoner's
legs until the length neared its end just above
Foss's knees and he was forced to finish off with
some very strong-looking knots. 'That should do
it,' he said, inspecting his work minutely and
appearing satisfied. 'I'm a good hand at this kind
of thing. Besides, Foss is in no state to perform
prodigies.'

'He's suffering from concussion,' Jake Kildare
agreed, 'and could even have been hurt
internally.'

'I think he'll last for as long as we need him.'
Tuffnel said. 'But there's no profit in discussing
him here. We have other business, do we not?'

Frowning, Jake Kildare gave his head a single
emphatic jerk.

Foss knew that they were about to depart, and
he was suddenly conscious of being very thirsty.
'Do a man a favour,' he said. 'I'm parched. Give me
a drink of water before you go away.'

Kildare and Tuffnel looked surprised, startled
even – or possibly nonplussed – as if he had
turned up some inner secret of theirs in the
innocence of his request, and they gazed at each
other for a long moment and burst out laughing.
After that, to Foss's stunned bewilderment now,
they turned away and left him, and he soon found

himself licking his lips in complete darkness, knowing that he had been denied and wondering how fellow human beings could have shrugged off his need with such evident pleasure. If it had been only that. For he could not help suspecting that there had indeed been something more involved.

Foss closed his eyes. He had the inner light of his imagination to live by, and his thirst was no great torment as yet. He could still think of other things. Brian Tuffnel and Jake Kildare had him puzzled. They had not mentioned Helen by name, and yet he was all too aware that they were planning to kill her. How did they intend to do it? And what was his part in it to be? Since he was certain that he had been given a role. Had it been otherwise, he would have been slain before now and his mortal parts disposed of where they would never be found. He was dealing with real evil here – a force as subtle and intelligent as the power of hell itself – and he would only stand a chance against it if he realized every moment of the time that it revelled in the worst and would do it always without the least hesitation.

The air in the mine was heavy, and the darkness oppressed. Foss felt in his impotence that he must do something – must try to combat unseen events by one means or another; and, weak though he was, he gathered what strength he could and fought his bonds, but this only made him feel worse than ever, for no turn of the ropes yielded even fractionally to his muscular striving. So, full of renewed agonies and nearing his last gasp, he gave up the struggle and sank into a deep sleep which could have been a faint.

He came to abruptly, and seemed blind as he opened his eyes to the dark. The silence actually roared in his ears, and panic threatened. No longer did he have a sense of time. Outside the moon could have set or the dawn broken, yet there was no measure of the hours in any portion of his being. Perhaps, though, his thirst was the natural yardstick, for it was now a cruel one and his throat seemed to be closing up in the rough heat of it. His captors had been gone a long time – and might never return. And here came the most frightening thought of all! He and the dark could become one. He might never know the moment of his death, and believe himself still alive as his mouldering bones fell apart. Indeed, a man had to scare himself to be truly afraid.

Then he heard something, and the strained ambience about him settled back to normal. He listened hard. Yes, he had picked up a faint echo of movement from away to his left. Now he heard feet approaching along the main gallery, and the presence of a faint glow impinged upon his blindness. The sounds grew louder, and the brightness increased – and suddenly he was caught in the middle of what seemed to be a glaring ray and glimpsed shapes advancing into his own tunnel behind it.

'I see you're still here, Foss!' Brian Tuffnel's voice mocked. 'Jake and I have brought you some company. We have my dear half-sister with us. You like her, don't you?'

'Pipsqueak!' Foss gritted, irritated by the

other's jeering patronage. 'If you're a good example of breeding and education, I'd rather be ignorant!'

'You're certainly that,' Brian Tuffnel agreed humourlessly. 'What would you know about breeding and education? Your kind exists only to serve mine!' He placed the lantern which he was holding on the ground to his left. 'Put her down, Jake.'

Foss's eyes were now quickly adjusting to what was after all only a soft glow of light through the lantern's rather sooty glass, and he watched the figure of Jake Kildare come stooping into view. The big man had his niece laid across his shoulders, and he unloaded Helen none too gently upon the ground, where she came to rest bound and inert near the male captive's feet. The girl was plainly unconscious, but appeared unharmed in any real sense, and Foss instantly suspected that she had been drugged, for he detected a faint medicinal odour from the region of her mouth and was fairly sure that he had smelled it once or twice before around sickrooms. 'You fiends!' he raged, unable to control himself in the near madness of the moment. 'You pair of mean, murdering hellions! May every curse that was ever uttered fall upon you two!'

Tuffnel rounded sharply. He kicked Foss hard in the ribs; then said: 'You seem to misunderstand the situation, Foss. If there's a murderer present, you are the man. You have just kidnapped this poor girl from her bed. And all because she told you some home truths and fired you! Tomorrow –

today – you will both die, and when your bodies are found and what has happened is fully understood, it will be the name of Ben Foss that goes forever accursed.'

'Just what the hell are you devils up to?' Foss ground out. 'If you've got to kill us, kill us clean and have done!'

'And perhaps hang for it?' Tuffnel tut-tutted. 'What a simple mind you have! We intend to live long and enjoy our crimes to the full. Blame there has to be, and you'll take it. What are we up to? You'll see shortly. When you do, you'll realize why men like us are born to so much and you to so little.'

Foss had the words, and once more he attempted a hot retort, but his mouth and throat were now so dry that only an angry croak passed his lips.

'Thirsty?' Tuffnel inquired.

Foss licked his dry lips with a leathery tongue and didn't try to deny it.

'You shall drink before long,' Tuffnel promised, making a sign to his companion; and once again he and Jake Kildare turned away laughing.

Foss still didn't get it, but felt that he ought to.

TEN

Again Foss sat in darkness, but it was as if the totality of it no longer had any effect on him. The recent presence of light seemed to have broken the black spell completely, though the concentration on his thirst had magnified that tenfold. He tried to ease his dryness by sucking at his salivary glands – since he didn't feel his body should be that arid as yet – but nothing helped, and his only relief from his own plight came in worrying about the girl who lay unconscious at his feet. But that was really no more than exchanging one form of distress for another.

He wondered in moments of forgetfulness where Brian Tuffnel and Jake Kildare had gone; but, whereas they had obviously returned to the Circle K ranch house on leaving him last, he felt pretty sure that this time they were lingering close by and adding the finishing touches to whatever evil they had planned for the day. Aside from that, of course, they could be resting or simply waiting for the sun. For he still had no reliable idea of what the time was.

Helen stirred. Fearing what her reaction might

be if she left a sleeping nightmare for one of the waking variety, he put the soles of his boots against her body and pressed hard a couple of times, but his effort was lost when the very thing that he feared seemed to happen and she began to scream. 'Helen!' he pleaded, pressing repeatedly now. 'Easy, girl! It's Ben! I'm here, honey!'

He kept trying, but she kept screaming, and it was obvious that his attempts to comfort her were either not impressing her mind or actually going unheard. He imagined it could well be the latter, for she was probably suspended between her drugged state and a reality that she could not recognize as such. Total darkness was very hard to take, as hadn't he found out. Even on a night without stars, some little thing would occasionally glint and provide an assurance that the normal world was still present. But the blackness within the earth could be mistaken for that of the grave.

Presently the girl became quiet. It seemed that she had exhausted herself. Foss made fresh efforts to communicate with her, both by words and touch, but was still unsuccessful, and he was at last forced to the conclusion that she had lapsed into unconsciousness again. He hoped this was so. There could be no doubt that she was more sensitive than most, and her level of suffering had been too high. An experience like this could bring on an illness that might last for years. Always supposing that she was fortunate enough to live past today.

A lot more time went by, possibly an hour or two. Then new footfalls out in the main gallery heralded the second return of Tuffnel and Kildare. The two men, once more illumined by the glow from their lantern, looked tired but determined as they turned into the side tunnel where the prisoners lay. Big Jake picked up Helen again and, more or less ignoring Foss, the two villains turned and went back the way they had come. This left the male prisoner with fresh doubts as to what they were scheming on, but he was not left long to his uncertainties, for they reappeared after ten minutes or so, and Tuffnel, who was carrying an uncorked canteen, knelt at Foss's side and put the bottle to his lips. 'Drink,' he encouraged. 'I know you're thirsty. Drink as much as you like!'

The invitation stirred a vague suspicion in Foss's mind, but he was too thirsty to dwell upon it. He filled his mouth and swallowed – knowing the folly of that too – then drank greedily, Tuffnel giving him every assistance, and his body seemed to soak up the liquid as drought-stricken soil absorbed the rain. In fact he must have gulped down the better part of a pint before emergent wind forced him to turn his head aside and belch; and, relieved, he would have gone on to empty the canteen, but just then Jake Kildare put out a staying hand and said sharply: 'That's enough, Brian!' And it was only as Tuffnel withdrew the waterbottle from his reach and corked it that Foss realized the water had had a faint odour to it and a slight bitterness that was now clinging to his tongue.

'Are you sure he didn't have too much, Jake?'

Tuffnel suddenly asked, face turned back across his right shoulder. 'You did say it was a fairly weak mixture and to let him have plenty.'

'I think he's taken about the right amount,' Jake Kildare answered. 'We don't want him falling asleep on us. It was a different matter with the girl.'

'Have you poisoned me?' Foss asked. 'What have I been given?'

'Only a solution of chloral hydrate,' Kildare replied. 'Just enough to confuse you and upset your judgement. You'll feel it before long. Don't be afraid! It's really quite pleasant.'

'The widow's nightcap,' Foss muttered, already feeling the edges of his mind getting fuzzy. 'What are you s.o.b.'s scheming?'

'Untie his legs, Brian,' Jake Kildare ordered, 'and let's get him on his feet. The earlier we get this job done, the less chance of anybody being around to see us.'

Tuffnel removed the rope from Foss's legs. This took a minute or two and, by the time it was done, Foss was beginning to feel light-headed and to see everything through a haze. The two men hauled him erect, and he ought to have been stricken with cramp, but his muscles had become so relaxed that he found he could stand without difficulty and even shuffle along as required by the steadying hands on his arms.

Kildare and Tuffnel guided him out of the side passage and into the main. They headed now for the eastern exit from the excavation. Foss felt quite exhilarated. Short of harming him, his captors seemed to have done him a favour. But in his real self, while prepared to enjoy his improved state of well-being, he knew better than that.

They left the mine via the cavemouth. Outside, Foss found himself half blinded by the soft golden glow of the newly risen sun – and he almost wished that he were back in the dark – but his eyesight quickly adjusted as they descended the slope towards the grass below, and he was able to see more or less normally when they reached the bottom.

Foss saw the horse and cart from the ranch once more, and the horses belonging to his captors were again secured to its tailgate. Helen Kildare was sitting in the back of the vehicle. Foss realized now that she was clad only in her nightdress; but, though she had sagged forward in her bonds – so that her forehead rested on her knees – he had the impression that she had regained consciousness; and this was suddenly proved when she seemed to hear the men approaching and looked up quickly, her hair spilling over her shoulders and her eyes glassy and out of focus. 'Ben!' she rubbered out. 'I'm sorry, Ben!'

He thought she must be talking about her lack of response in the mine, and supposed she must have been aware of more that had taken place than he imagined, but he shook his head and made it plain that whatever was worrying her didn't matter.

'Let's get him into the cart,' Jake Kildare urged, as they neared the vehicle. 'He's quite capable of climbing that wheel if we steady him.'

They halted beside the cart and, held in place
by the two men at his back, Foss climbed the
spokes of the near side wheel and accepted the
push which sent him tumbling into the transport's buck, where he came to rest on his left side
and had managed to work himself into a sitting
position by the time that Tuffnel and Kildare had
climbed onto the driving board and the former
picked up the reins.

There was a slap of the leathers. 'Walk on!'
Tuffnel ordered irritably; and the horse jerked the
cart into motion and went plodding northwards –
into country which Foss had supposed to be sealed
off by the grass ridges of the area; but he soon
discovered that his captors knew the terrain
better than he, for presently Tuffnel drove round
the back of some brush – where no path appeared
to be – and Foss saw the sandy bed of a dried-up
stream that threaded a deep cleft between two
eminences and emerged in green country beyond,
the way through effectively invisible until the
traveller was actually upon it.

They traversed the great fissure without
difficulty and, with its gloom behind them, the
happily befuddled Foss realized that, though he
had long worked close to it, they were now
actually rolling across land which he had never
seen before, and that the steep, hollowed upturn
of the ground not far ahead ended in a long,
grassy ridge which had been just another feature
of the nearer country up to now. Half inclined to
comment on his surprise at this, Foss glanced
round at Kildare and Tuffnel – but he could see

that they would clearly have no interest in anything that he might say – and, as Helen remained dazed and speechless in all that mattered, he let his undoubtedly foolish impulse pass and the journey continue unremarked, suspecting that it would prove a rather short one anyhow.

And it did. For it ended in fact at the top of the climb that he had seen before them. Now he had a dizzying view of a huge basin on his left that sank into the earth for a thousand feet and more, had every kind of jagged mass and rock-pile tumbled across its floor, and was approached from the present vantage by a steep path – which was indeed little more than a narrow, jutting ledge – that followed the settling cliff-face downwards until it spilled off at the bottom into places hidden by the terrain from this elevation.

'There you are, Foss,' Tuffnel jested grimly. 'What you see before you is test enough for any man. How do you feel about driving a horse and cart down there?'

'Suicide!' Foss declared, doubting that the path was as wide as the vehicle in places.

'My word for it exactly,' Tuffnel drawled, smiling faintly as Jake Kildare climbed down from the cart, fetched his horse from the vehicle's rear, and then rode off down the narrow way.

'Where's he going to?' Foss demanded.

'None of your business!' Tuffnel responded. 'I'm going to untie you, Foss. After that you can pick up the reins and take that cart down the path. If you reach the bottom alive –' He shrugged. 'Who knows?'

'I know,' Foss mumbled, his tongue ballooning as the chloral numbed his brain. 'You intend for me to go over the edge. You expect me to crash that g'damned cart! Folk will say I killed Helen and myself all right. Is this your proof of why you're worth so much and I so little? Mister, this plan of yours isn't even manly!'

'So long as it works,' Tuffnel retorted, 'I don't care what it is. With you and Helen dead, Jake and I will have achieved what's necessary.' Spinning on his backside, he turned his feet over the driving board and set them down in the back of the cart, standing up then and bending towards Foss's bonds. 'Now shut up and let me get on with this.'

Foss looked down at himself, watching as Tuffnel untied the knots that held him. He knew that events were approaching a crisis, and that the anger he felt was only a small part of what he ought to be feeling. The drug in his system was dulling his emotions and slowing his reactions. He felt as incapable as an old man. The last of the rope loosened and fell away from him. His arms were free. He ought to be hitting out at Tuffnel or wrestling with the man, but all he could do was sit flopped in the bottom of the cart and watch as the other retreated to the vehicle's rear and freed his horse – jumping over the tailgate to the ground and then climbing into his saddle. 'Stir yourself!' he ordered, drawing a revolver from inside his jacket. 'Get into the driving seat!'

It was an effort, but Foss made it, blundering against the still benumbed Helen en route, and he straddled the driving board in a lurching movement and then thumped down upon it, ready to laugh like a fool at the absurdity of it all as he picked up the reins.

He was not even given a second longer to think about it. Tuffnel's gun banged. A tiny piece of hide flew off the pulling horse's neck. The animal gave a shrill neigh; then, panicking, it lunged into motion, dragging the cart after it into the broadest part of the descent at the top of the ledge. Standing up and using all his weight, Foss heaved on the reins, yelling at the brute to stop; but on the horse went, and the cart rumbled and swayed, chipping a boulder at the edge of the drop on the one hand and grinding out sparks and dust as the wheel hub made contact with the rock wall on the other.

Foss blinked at the road plunging ahead. He could see it pulsing there through a pinkish haze. Striving, he sought to make any small adjustment he could to keep the horse and vehicle near the middle of the narrow way, but he could already see the real hazards ahead – places where rocks pinched, holes gaped, and platelets of surface stone lay shattered and loose – and he had no idea how he was going to contend with those. The stampeding horse yanked at his shoulders, and he twisted the leathers around his wrists and forearms and put out all his strength in a final effort to control it, but the animal continued to chuck its mouth away from his directions and went on stretching downhill at full pace, fire springing up from under its hooves and pebbles

spitting out like shot from beneath the iron tyres
of the wheels and either flying into space or
pinging off the rock face on the right, some of
them to rattle against the cart itself.

It could get nothing but worse, and worse it got.
The sweat streaming off him, Foss sank back to
the driving board. They no longer seemed to be
rolling down the cliffside road so much as falling.
It amazed him that the cart – a clumsy enough
creation – had tracked accurately so far and
actually held together, since it was bouncing and
rocketing now and threatening to separate from
its tongue. Foss had visions of flying high, and
then dropping to oblivion on the cruel earth a
thousand feet below, but still he stayed with the
bouncing vehicle, the teeth jarring in his head and
his eyes no more than the organs of a dancing,
broken vision.

A very narrow spot seemed to advance on Foss
apace. It was obvious, even to his muddled senses,
that the road was inches less than wide enough to
carry the cart through safely. The wind buffeted
him, and dust blew into his face, as he waited for
the sudden lurch to the left which would
announce the beginning of the end, yet he saw the
vehicle's charmed life persist when the horse
veered to the right and brought the off side of the
cart into grinding contact with the bottom of an
overhang. This abrupt displacement seemed just
sufficient to keep half the near side wheel running
on the brink itself until the danger of the narrows
had swept by and the vehicle could race on into
the middle descent, bucking and jolting, and with

Helen now adding her screams to the snorting of the horse and the profanities which the petrified Foss uttered at each new joint-dislocating heave and bang.

The potholes were numerous here. Sometimes the cart bounced to the left, and sometimes to the right. Smashed wheel-bearings shrilled now, casting out blue and malodorous smoke, and bolts clattered and fell to the road as they sheared. Bits of wood also started to shake off the buck. Other 'almost' disasters came and went, subject to the same swooping violence, and then debris, no doubt displaced by the vibrations, began to rain down from above. Foss sat through it all, still waiting for the end; and, by this stage, he found it almost incredible to believe in what he had seen. He and Helen ought to have been pitched into space a dozen times; yet, with the cart threatening to turn into a wreck and he well aware that they had survived this far thanks to no virtue of his own, he began to think that they were going to come through their impossible plunge, for the last part of the tight cliffside road was now opening ahead of them and he could see level places among the rock-piles immediately below.

Foss heaved on the reins again. He seemed to get some response from a pulling horse that was calming as exhaustion sapped it. The headlong rush slowed perceptibly. But it was not to be that easy. His enemies had anticipated the possibility of the present miracle, and Foss now learned why Jake Kildare had gone on ahead – for the big man suddenly sprang out of a bay at the roadside and

into the path of the oncoming horse and cart.
There he danced, a fist pumping above his head
while he used the other hand to fire pistol shots
into the air.

This latest shock was too much for the pulling
horse. It snatched sharply away to the left, and
Foss knew that this time it must go over the
precipice. Now everything seemed to happen at
once. Amidst all the grinding noise and the
irresistible force of the slewing motion, Foss heard
a shot, and Jake Kildare was struck to the ground
and then lay very still. But Foss had no more than
his fleeting glimpse of that, for he was suddenly
rocketing upwards as the cart snapped its tongue
and angled sharply back to the right, bowling
onwards to crash into the upper side of the bay
from which Jake Kildare had recently appeared,
the force of the impact propelling Helen out of the
cart's back as the tailgate sprang from its
pinnings and fell to the ground. The girl came to
rest in the dust at the side of the road.

Foss felt himself reach the top of his climb and
begin dropping. He was aware of the gulf and the
horse plunging to certain death below him. There
seemed an inevitability about it all. But his
instincts were still alive and, realizing in a split
second that he would be falling very near the edge
of the jutting ledge which carried the road down
the cliffside, he flung out his hands, grabbing
frantically at the brink – and his fingers held and
his body slammed in hard against the face of the
precipice, yet not hard enough to hurt him badly
or dislodge his grip.

He hung there, panting. There was in him a cold fear of slipping away into the emptiness beneath his feet, and a terror also that he no longer had the strength to haul himself to safety across the slight overhang of the brink. But he gathered himself, backed his muscular power with the force of his will, and began to drag himself upwards across the edge, bowing his face into the dirt as his nose slid towards the point at which he would know that he had broken the power of gravity over his lower body and was safe in all that mattered.

Then, to his amazed horror, a foot came to rest on his left shoulder and a powerful shove sent him sliding backwards over the brink again and into the hanging position that he had occupied before. An awful dismay filled him, but he hung on tightly and, looking up, saw the darkly handsome face of Brian Tuffnel – who must have galloped his horse down the cliffside path behind the cart – grinning down at him sadistically. Now the young man stepped right up to the brink and placed the soles of his boots on the knuckles of Foss's clinging hands. He ground at the finger bones, increasing the weight employed with every moment, and an excruciating pain filled the hanging man's hands and arms.

Jaws clenched, Foss matched his will against Tuffnel's, but it wasn't so much the pain which he needed to endure as the numbness in his grip that he now had to combat. All the feeling would go out of his fingers before long and the muscles of his hands automatically relax. His suspended form

would then go slipping away into space and he
would die on the rocks far below. The vision of it
made him hang on harder than ever.

Suddenly Tuffnel frowned. Against the likeli-
hood he seemed to concede. Stepping back a little,
he aimed the revolver that he was holding down
into Foss's face, slowly thumbing back the
hammer as he did so, and the hanging man waited
to exchange what would have been a quick death
for an instant one. But, before Tuffnel could
squeeze the trigger, a rifle boomed from close by to
his left. Drawing up in a startled manner, he
looked towards the explosion – an expression of
pique and outrage coming to his features as he
saw who had shot him – and then he tumbled over
the brink and plunged towards the floor of the
basin far below.

Swearing in his very best manner, to keep his
courage up, Foss gathered himself anew and,
hardly knowing how he managed it, dragged
himself back over the brink for the second time.
On this occasion, his nose ploughed through the
dust to a point far beyond that at which safety
might be adjudged and he finally allowed his
suffering shape to flatten upon the cliffside road
and rest from its ordeal.

ELEVEN

Before long Foss was conscious of two people gazing down at him. He looked up to see a freed Helen and her mother standing there. Rita Kildare was gaunt and looked stricken at the heart. She held a Winchester in her hands, and Foss had no doubt that it was the rifle which had shot both Jake Kildare and the woman's son. 'But you loved the boy, ma'am,' he said, the question mark audible in his voice as he got back to his feet. 'You loved them both.'

'Yes,' Mrs Kildare agreed. 'But what's more, I deserved them. They'd have destroyed me and each other in the end. The Circle K would have wasted too. I knew the worst when I heard them come like thieves in the night and spirit my daughter away. I realized that they had murder on their minds, but I could only follow them – and pray. I hoped nobody would have to die, but somebody had to at the last, for there was no other way. So was it to be the innocent or the guilty? Guilty as I am, I chose to save the innocent. Now I can only say sorry and ask you to forgive me for helping bring matters to this pass. The words seem hopelessly inadequate' – she shook her head – 'and the situation lacking real logic. I feel myself beyond forgiveness.'

'No, you're not, mother!' Helen said warmly, seeming almost her normal self again and carrying only a graze and a bruise or two to mark her violent ejection from the back of the crashed cart. 'You were led astray by your own heart. You're not old, and you still wanted a life for yourself. Those two wicked men knew it, and they exploited you. In your circumstances, anybody might have made the wrong choice, mother!'

'No,' Rita Kildare said, shaking her head. 'I made my choice deliberately. Had Jake and Brian been less evil than they were, I might have stood by it – and this morning had a very different outcome. I deserve to be punished, and no punishment is really too bad for me.'

'At that, you've nothing to be proud of,' Foss said. 'But you're also being a mite hard on yourself. Jake and your boy were their own men – with their own course mapped out – and Helen and I would be dead as mutton but for you. The threat to the Circle K is also lifted. Everything can get back to normal this very day.'

'I charge you with it, Ben Foss,' Helen informed him. 'You've been the real boss around the place since dad died, and I didn't mind a bit.'

'That's it,' Rita Kildare said. 'You two get on with it. If I don't end up in prison, I'm going away shortly.'

'We'll see you don't end up in prison,' Foss assured her.

'The ranch will seem so – so empty without you there, mother,' Helen pleaded.

'Well,' the older woman said, 'you two are just the age to take care of that.'

Foss rubbed his nose and grinned to himself. He could see the look Helen was giving him and was ready to play his part.

He cleared his throat. 'Jake and Tuffnel have left horses to spare. I'll round them up. Then let's go home.'